A
Harlequin
Romance

OTHER
Harlequin Romances
by KATRINA BRITT

THE HOUSE CALLED SAKURA

by

KATRINA BRITT

HARLEQUIN BOOKS   TORONTO
WINNIPEG

Original hard cover edition published in 1974
by Mills and Boon Limited.

© Katrina Britt 1974

SBN 373-01892-4

Harlequin edition published July 1975

Printed in Canada

1892

CHAPTER ONE

SLOWLY, the mist lifted and the sea which hitherto had been a choppy grey changed miraculously to an enchanting blue, giving Laurel an exciting glimpse of Fujiyama as the ship approached the superb harbour. Oriental sampans came into view, their decks alive with slanting-eyed, yellow-skinned little men.

Then the big ships from foreign ports mingling with those flying the flag of the Rising Sun. From the deck of the ship, Laurel's first impression of Japan was that of a lovely siren gaily executing the dance of the seven veils.

Provocatively, tantalizingly, she discarded them one by one to reveal scenes of incredible beauty, each one more lovely than the last. Lightly, the veils of gauze mist were tossed away on the breeze to frolic and curve around the branches of pine trees gracing the delicate lines of the hills now touched to gold by the sun.

Laurel could feel its warmth through her linen suit as it blazed down on to the innumerable islands caressed lovingly by the inland sea. On one oasis of greenery a beautiful old temple pricked the blue sky in isolated splendour with the liberating breeze whisked away the last of the misty veils to frolic around the fishing fleet setting out in full sail.

Their junk sails, held together by intricate interlacing of ropes, strained against the breeze, a picturesque craft gliding over the surface of the water like silver veined butterflies on blue glass.

The scene photographed itself on Laurel's mind with an endearing clarity. Everything was so fresh, so young, so gay, so utterly different from anything she had ever seen that she found herself smiling at the yellow faces beneath mushroom hats bobbing up and down industriously between bales of rice straw on the quay.

With quickening heartbeats she scanned the crowd awaiting the ship's arrival and the heat rose in her cheeks. There he was! A wild thrill shot through her. He had not changed. He was still larger than life with a careless grace about him, a quality which, while it arrested and charmed, also gave confidence. He looked tanned and very fit, unlike Laurel, who was pale, tired and a little overwhelmed upon reaching a country that alternately charmed and frightened her by its strangeness.

The sun glinted upon the crisp tobacco-brown hair combed back from an intelligent forehead as the keen grey eyes, inscrutable beneath straight dark brows, pinpointed her slender figure. The lean sardonic face relaxed suddenly into a white smile which gave the well cut mouth and slightly hooked masculine nose a boyish look. But there was nothing boyish about Kirk Graham. He was a man in complete control of his own destiny. It showed in his arrogant stance, the proud bearing and the nonchalant wave of a firm brown hand, Laurel thought, as she fluttered her small one in greeting.

Even from a distance with the blue water still dividing them, she felt his magnetism. Suddenly she trembled with the realization that she was shy of this man who was soon to become her husband. Was it only a year since their first meeting, a year in which her life had so irrevocably changed? The crowd of unfamiliar faces swam before her eyes. It all came back as clearly as though it had happened yesterday.

It had been one of those days for Laurel, that fateful day when she had decided to springclean the lounge of the cottage. Every-

6

thing had gone wrong from the moment she had stripped the room to wipe down ceiling and walls. It had developed into one of her mother's off days and, to make matters worse, the doctor had been late calling. Laurel had finished the room and had been about to hang the freshly laundered summer curtains when he had called.

After he had gone, she had rushed out with the prescription, hoping to reach the chemist in the village before closing time. It had been essential for her mother to have the newly prescribed drug, for the previous one had made her feel sick and ill.

Evidently, the doctor had not had a good day either, for he was well over an hour late finishing his rounds and the cottage had been his last place of call before driving home to evening surgery. Pity he had been going in the opposite direction or Laurel could have asked him for a lift to the village. A glance at her watch told her she had just a quarter of an hour to reach the chemist before closing time at five-thirty. Failing that meant going to the next chemist on the rota for late night closing at Sabridge five miles away. Of course the car had refused to start, and in exasperation at all that had gone before, Laurel had set off to walk the considerable distance to the village.

She had hurried out just as she was in jeans and workaday top, her dark hair covered by a gay scarf. Half walking, half running, she had not seen one chink of light in the black clouds hanging over her since the train accident which had cost her father his life and her mother severe head injuries.

She had been so engrossed in her troubles that the long sleek car approaching had pulled up smoothly beside her before she was aware of it.

"Excuse me. I'm looking for Doctor Machelle. I believe he lives somewhere in the vicinity."

The charming cultured voice had come from a dark well-shaped head emerging from the open car window. Laurel, gasping for breath, had stopped precipitately, torn between hurrying on and helping this stranger. Her small firm bust had risen and fallen agitatedly as she pictured the chemist putting up his shutters because of the delay.

"Oh dear!" Her words came out in a rush. "I'm in a dreadful hurry and it's rather complicated to explain. You keep straight on . . ."

She had broken off abruptly. The man's eyes, grey as steel in a suntanned face, held an amused twinkle.

"Is someone chasing you or are you going some place?" he drawled, taking in her slim figure and the scarf tied nursewise on her head.

"I'm going to the chemist in the village and he'll close at any moment. Where was I?"

Slowly he had released the catch on the car door and opened it. "You were telling me how to find my uncle George. Hop in and you can tell me on the way to the chemist."

There had been a kindling appraisal in his look and his manner had been kindly in a way that instilled confidence. Laurel, piteously in need of a helping hand, had stammered, "But ... but it will be taking you out of your way. You must have just come from there."

"I have. Shall we go back?"

She had wondered afterwards why her embarrassment had fallen away as she complied. She had taken an awful risk accepting a lift from a comparative stranger whose gorgeous tan could not possibly have been acquired through the rigours of an English winter. Had it not been for the almost imperceptible air of aloofness behind the grey eyes, she would never have accepted. As it was she had sunk into the luxurious upholstery to give him a steady look.

His profile had presented the outline of a Roman gladiator

8

who had attained near perfection in everything he had undertaken. His air of alertness, his immaculate city-going suit, his firm hands on the wheel of the car coaxing it to speed had mesmerized her.

"Well, is the summing up satisfactory?"

He had continued to keep his eyes front as if to spare her any further embarrassment.

Touched, Laurel had given a little chuckle, completely reassured.

"I might not be a very good judge of character, but I'm not worried."

"Thanks. I can usually be relied upon, although, as they say, self-praise is no recommendation."

He had smiled at her then, a smile that was somehow breathtaking. It had reminded Laurel that not only was her face minus make-up but she was also dishevelled and very tired. She had told him everything about her parents' accident with the feeling that he had a right to know. He had listened gravely without comment until she had finished.

"So you're left to pick up the pieces, as it were," had been his brief observation. "Hard luck on your own. Poor child!"

The chemist had been on the verge of closing when they had arrived and in a short time Laurel was back in the car with the precious prescription.

"Lovely day," her companion had remarked when they had left the village behind.

Laurel had agreed, feeling the heat of the sun through the car windows. Wretchedly sticky, she had longed for a leisurely bath, realizing her foolishness in trying to cram all the work into one day.

No wonder her head had throbbed from sheer exhaustion. But she had managed to give him the directions to the doctor's residence.

9

"Thank you. You've been very kind," she had told him as he drew up the car at the gate of the cottage

"So have you," he had replied with his smile slowly changing to a frown of concern on seeing her pale, strained little face. "Are you all right?"

"Yes, thanks. It's been a warm day for working. Goodbye and thanks again."

Somewhat unsteadily, Laurel had been leaving the car when the ground had suddenly rushed up and hit her. She had opened her eyes to find herself lying in a chair in front of the uncurtained window in the lounge where she had toiled so laboriously all that day in between looking after her mother.

He had been standing slightly to one side of her chair chafing her hands while allowing the fresh air from the open window to reach her. With a swift cry of distress Laurel had looked up into the grey eyes watching her so intently .

"Oh, dear!" she had cried. "Did I pass out? I've never done that before in my life."

"It's all right. Lie still." His tone and touch had been absolutely gentle but firm when she had tried weakly to sit up. "I'm going to make you a cup of tea."

And because she had felt so utterly exhausted and ill Laurel, had leaned her aching head back against the cushions he had thrust behind her and closed her eyes. She had opened them again when he had entered the room with the tea tray.

The sunlight from the uncurtained window had given a coppery sheen to his crisp dark hair. It was the kind that curls when wet and his eyes were the sort that danced when he smiled. He was, as far as she could judge, on the outer rim of his twenties, which accounted for his mature looks. Looking at him had made her heart feel as light as her head.

"I managed to find everything in the kitchen," he said, placing the tray on a low table and carrying it near to her chair.

Adding milk to a dainty eggshell china cup in gold and yellow, he proceeded to pour out the tea. "My guess is you've been working without a break. Now be sensible and drink this."

It was much stronger than she liked it and he had dropped three cubes of sugar into the cup before handing it to her. Laurel had closed her eyes and drunk it gratefully, ignoring her revulsion of sugar in her tea. Then he was handing her the home-made shortbread she kept in a biscuit tin colourfully painted with Japanese geisha girls.

She had taken one to please him after insisting that he poured out a cup of tea for himself.

"Ever been to Japan?" he had queried with the quirk of a dark brow at the tin as he took a shortbread. She shook her head and he went on, "It's a delightful country."

He had a deep vibrating voice and he spoke in clear precise English. Listening to him, Laurel forgot the lounge window minus curtains and the cup of tea she had intended taking up to her mother before bringing her downstairs for tea. She had learned that his name was Kirk Graham. He was thirty-one and was a secretary at the British Embassy in Tokyo. He had been on vacation with another six weeks to go and had decided to look up his uncle George, known to Laurel as Doctor Machelle. They had been deep in conversation when Laurel's mother had walked in with a hostile expression in her blue eyes.

Kirk had risen immediately as she had entered the room and Laurel, who had now fully recovered, went to meet her.

"Darling," she said, taking her mother's arm, "I'm awfully sorry to have forgotten your cup of tea, but I've managed to get your new prescription, thanks to Mr. Kirk Graham here who so kindly gave me a lift to the village before the chemist closed."

Laurel had introduced them and Leila Stewart had acknowledged Kirk's greeting in a clear soft voice. The blue eyes, once so warm and eloquent, were blank. She returned her smile without really smiling. Laurel had gently taken her mother to a chair, choking back the tears and wishing that the charming stranger had known her real mother and not this broken, joyless woman sterile with memories. She had been such a poppet.

To her surprise Kirk had seemed to understand. Charmingly, he plied her mother with tea and shortbread There was no mention of Laurel's collapse. Leila had lost the capacity to hold any information long enough in her mind for her poor bruised brain to assimilate. Her eyes had regarded him blankly, taking in the immaculate suit, the hand-made soft leather shoes and his well-groomed appearance accentuated by his charm.

For his part, Kirk had seen a woman as slim and dainty as a girl of twenty-five with blue eyes and brown hair untouched with grey. But her cream and rose complexion was marred by the scar which meandered from her hair across her forehead and down her cheek. The tailored simplicity of her soft beige dress had given her an air of delicacy and charm. He had been enchanted to find himself in the company of two of the most charming women it had been his pleasure to meet since arriving in England. They had talked, what about Laurel could never have remembered. But she did remember Kirk's keen eyes taking in the curtains she had been in the act of putting up when the doctor had called. Taking them from the back of the chair where she had left them, he had put them up, making short work of it with his long arms.

After that he had called every day at the cottage to take them out for a run in his car sometimes to the coast where Laurel had bathed with him in the sea while her mother had sat on the beach. He had borrowed his uncle's boat and had taken them both for a sail or he had dined with them at the cottage.

Laurel had prepared chicken delicately golden, tender sliced young beans, small new potatoes and fresh young green peas

12

from the kitchen garden. She had felt ridiculously pleased when he had asked for a second helping of her apple strudel. Sometimes in his company her mother had responded to his wit and charm before the shutter came down again over her face and it had taken again a heartbreaking blankness.

Laurel, whose energy had been tapped until there had been no reserves by the shock of her father's death and the constant attention on her mother, had been recharged by Kirk's vitality. She had discovered that he was an excellent golfer, getting up at six in the morning to play on the links with his uncle George before breakfast. He was also a strong swimmer and took a delight in driving at speed.

When he had gone back to London after a month's stay at his uncle's, Laurel had ached for a sight of him. Then the letter had arrived in his strong masculine scrawl inviting them both up to London for the last week of his leave. Her joy had known no bounds. He had booked them in at a hotel, and that week was one Laurel would never forget. They had gone to shows, art galleries, visited parks, dined in all the smart places. She had danced with him in the intimate glow of dimly lit luxurious places until she had not been herself any more.

She had become hopelessly lost in his charms, his low chuckle, his casual easy acceptance of the best wherever they went, his sense of humour, congenital courtesy and slow tantalizing smile. All these and his unfailing kindness and attention to her mother had bound her heart in silken cords, imprisoning it against all comers.

That last night in London when he had delivered them to their hotel rooms he had taken her aside when her mother had gone to her room. Keen-eyed, he had looked down into her flushed face.

"I leave early tomorrow for Japan. I shall find a mountain of work awaiting me, so I shall be busy for the next few weeks.

I'll give you my address and I want your promise to write to me." From the pocket of his dinner jacket Kirk had given her an envelope with his address and had pressed it into her hand. "Will you write?"

Laurel had been near to tears. She had known that when he had gone she would die a little. He had been her knight errant, riding in a sleek black car instead of on a white charger. Now he was going away for ever out of her life. She had looked up at him, valiantly hiding her feelings. I love everything about him, she had thought despairingly, his leashed energy, his outrageous charm and devastating smile and the way he has walked into my life to give it a new meaning. He had seemed reluctant to leave her, putting a firm finger beneath her chin and lifting her face to his masterfully. The long hard kiss had continued despite the elderly couple who had come up in the lift to pass them on the corridor. Laurel had wanted to go on clinging to him, but her sense of delicacy prevented her. He had been very kind to her mother and to herself. It would not have been fair to mistake his courtesy and kindness for something more personal.

A man in Kirk's position and with his ability did not need a wife – at least not Laurel Stewart. He was quite capable of making a successful career without the help of a feminine hand. So Laurel had waited for him to write to her first before committing herself. His letters had been short because of the pressure of work. Then, gradually, they had lengthened, demanding all her news in return.

But Laurel had not told him that her mother had grown worse and had become violent at intervals. The injury to her head had resulted in a piece of bone penetrating her brain. An operation had been out of the question and Laurel had flatly refused to send her mother to hospital. When his proposal of marriage had come several months after he had gone back,

Laurel had read it through a mist of tears. It had taken a few days of sleepless torment and many sheets of writing paper before she finally wrote her refusal.

The months following had taxed her strength and courage to the utmost. Doctor Machelle was away on a course and without Kirk's letters to sustain her Laurel became a shadow of her former self. Scenes with her mother when, for no apparent reason, she would throw the first thing on hand at Laurel had become a nightmare. The climax had come on the day Doctor Machelle returned. He had called at the cottage with his locum to see how his patient was. They had found Laurel unconscious and bleeding profusely from a wound in her temple. She was lying on the floor of her mother's room not far away from the silver candelabrum which her mother had thrown at her.

Leila Stewart died that night, and Laurel lay for weeks in a twilight world. Doctor Machelle had taken her to his home in the care of his housekeeper. And gradually she began to gain strength. When she was strong enough the doctor sent her to a cottage in Cornwall where she was looked after by an old aunt of his. She was there when Kirk sent a second proposal of marriage.

Laurel had carried the letter back home with her to the cottage unanswered. While she longed with all her heart to go out to him something seemed to be holding her back from answering the letter. His uncle George approached her in his forthright way in the end, telling her he knew of the proposal and that he was taking care of all the arrangements to get her away.

With her feelings in cold storage, she had bought her trousseau after sending Kirk her acceptance of his proposal, and now here she was on the deck of the ship bringing her nearer to the man who had taken her heart for all time. Nervously, Laurel tugged at her white gloves, adjusted her shoulder bag

15

and glanced down at her neat navy suit and white court shoes. All unnecessary actions, she knew, like patting the Grecian-styled coils of hair when not a hair was out of place.

By the time the ship docked, her heart was hammering against her ribs and her mouth was dry. Then she was holding out her hands to him and looking up into his face with the tears running down her cheeks.

He gripped her hands before drawing her against him with a look of concern. "Eh, now! I hope those are tears of happiness."

He dealt swiftly with the tears and the handkerchief was back in his pocket as taking her arms in his strong hands he looked down into her pale face. To her tired spirit he was the embodiment of youth, strength and vitality bringing with him a fresh tang of mountain air mingling pleasingly with the masculine fragrance of good grooming. He was even more devastating at close quarters than she remembered and it made her feel weak just to look at him.

"Are you better, my sweet? You look tired. I hope the journey hasn't proved too much for you."

He bent his head then to kiss her cheek like a brother might have done. It occurred to her then that his uncle George had been keeping him well informed.

She gave a pale smile. "I'm much better. I'm going to love Japan. It gives an impression of being all fun and gaiety. I feel I want to laugh and cry at the same time."

He watched the frank enchantment of her face. "And are you pleased to see me?" he whispered.

Laurel trembled as she stared up at his dark features and firm leanness, trying to believe he still loved her, a woman who had been remote and almost a stranger for so long, a woman who must be persuaded to give herself unreservedly into his keeping, who would be expected to love him as he loved her.

16

It was all there mixed up in her mind. Giving him her love and trust would help her to restore her lost faith in life, in herself. Her need for him was like a searing pain.

Her smile was misty but ineffably sweet. "I've dreamed of nothing else."

Again she felt the spell of his magnetism, finding him as wonderful as at their first meeting. The look in her eyes must have convinced him, for his eyes softened as he looked down on her forlorn slim figure. From then on he took charge and to Laurel it was heaven.

If Yokohama had fascinated her, Tokyo filled her with delight. In Kirk's long sleek car they cruised along narrow winding streets past clusters of unpainted crazy warehouses and brown toy dwellings which actually housed families. Kirk told her that the Japanese did not favour painting their wooden houses. They believed that exposing the wood to the weather preserved it better.

The scene through her window was like a film – mushroom hats, gay kimonos, parasols and cotton trousers hurried along on bare feet in wooden clogs. They clip-clipped along the pavements to pause at open-air stalls overflowing with market produce, fish and household goods. Fat little babies nodded in sleep strapped on their mothers' backs and bicycles did miraculous curves around the traffic as the narrow shop-lined streets gave way to wide boulevards.

Here Europeans in western clothes mingled with the oriental kimonos and clogs. Presently, Kirk drew up at the New Otani Hotel where Laurel was to stay until her marriage. The foyer was filled with a happy, laughing, chattering throng of orientals in all their finery.

"A wedding party," Kirk whispered on their way to the reception desk. He took charge of her hotel key, ordered tea to be brought up and accompanied her to her rooms.

17

"Poor sweet, you looked tired out," was his comment. "We'll talk tomorrow when you've had a good night's sleep."

Laurel could have gone to sleep there and then, for Kirk had surrounded her with cushions in the bamboo chair in the Western-style room with its expanse of gleaming wood floor and the minimum of light unpolished furniture.

His lean capable fingers dispensed the Japanese green tea into small delicate cups from an enchanting teapot with a dragon's open mouth for the spout. She found the tea wonderfully refreshing and to please Kirk she ate two of the small cakes made from rice flour, a wafer-thin one flavoured with caraway seeds and vanilla-flavoured smothered in nuts.

The sense of strangeness slowly diminished. Kirk was as cool and managing as ever with that experienced look that defied things to go wrong. His smile was tolerant and teasing and at times grave and interested. Before he left her he stood looking down at her for a fleeting second and said with a crooked smile, "I'm still trying to convince myself that you're here." He bent his head to kiss her lips lightly. "I want you to go to bed now and rest. I'll be round in the morning. Sleep well, and dream of me."

Her heart soothed, Laurel found herself loving him as a reality far more than she had loved him as a fiancé far away. Being with him would take away all her sadness and sense of loss. He was hers now – or would be quite soon. How soon?

CHAPTER TWO

THAT night Laurel slept the sleep of exhaustion and awoke with a sense of strangeness to find her hotel room flooded with sunshine. The first thing in her thoughts was the wedding dress in her wardrobe. Kirk had not said how soon they were to be married. Was it possible that he had changed his mind since seeing her again? Laurel stared up at the ceiling with a scared feeling rippling along her nerves. Had Kirk changed in his feelings towards her since he had made his second proposal? After all, he met many beautiful women in his own circle of friends who would flock around him, drawn irresistibly by his charm and good looks, while she was just a shadow of her former self.

The thought of those women made her feel a wee bit sick at what was before her. Could she face up to meeting all his friends? Moreover, could she marry Kirk and be all that he expected in a wife? Cold sweat broke out like dew on her forehead and in putting up a pale little hand to her temple her fingers came into contact with the scar left by the blow from the candelabrum. A fraction of an inch to the left and the blow would have been fatal. But she had been spared, to be Kirk's wife. Her pulses hammered at the thought of being in his arms. She loved him – there was no doubt about that. Why then should she have the feeling of being hurried into something for which she was not quite ready? The loss of her parents had left her unsure and the world had become alien and frightening without their reassuring presence. Was that the reason?

Laurel had not found the answer when she left her bed to wash and dress. It occurred to her as she dressed her thick silken hair at the back of her head in the Grecian style which suited her so well that had her eyes been almond-shaped she could have passed for Japanese. Of medium height, she had the velvety skin of a camellia plus a delicacy of wrists and ankles that was pleasing. Moreover, the black silk flower-printed trouser suit in a size ten fitted her perfectly, outlining her softly rounded bust and tiny waist enchantingly. The low open neck revealed the slender column of her young throat and the enchanting curve of her chin. But her eyes were shadowed and her small face looked drawn.

Breakfast was brought to her room by a blandly smiling Japanese waiter – rolls, butter, honey, crisp toast and a boiled egg. The typically English breakfast ordered by Kirk the previous evening was set down on the lacquer table.

His knock on her door came around ten o'clock. Laurel rose with unspeakable relief from her enforced inactivity to open the door. He strode in with a bouquet of flowers, rosebuds with the dew still on them. His eyes, grey as steel in his tanned face, twinkled with amusement and more than a little appraisal at the pretty trouser suit before they narrowed on her flushed face and sweetly curving mouth.

"Good morning, my sweet. I bring you flowers when you're like a flower yourself. What are you, an English rose or a Japanese orchid?"

Laurel accepted the flowers with a feeling of agitation which she knew had to be checked before it came too apparent. She had been lucky that the breakdown she had suffered after her mother's death had only left her with frayed nerves which would heal with time.

"Both, I hope," she said, burying her face in the sweetness of the roses. "They're lovely. Thank you, Kirk."

20

She turned to place them down on the lacquer table and he looked down tenderly at her bent head.

"No kiss?"

Gently he turned her round to face him, his voice, his face, his lips a command as he bent his head.

Laurel trembled in his arms. The kisses of a year ago were never quite like this one. His lips were transmitting an electric current through her whole being, touching on every nerve in her body. She became glowingly alive and her whole being responded to his nearness. She clung, and it was Kirk who drew away. His grey eyes met hers fully for a breathtaking moment in a look which made her quickly lower her own.

He spoke, she thought, a trifle unsteadily for him. "I mustn't forget that you're still not a hundred per cent fit."

Subduing the wild beating of her heart, she said breathlessly, "I'm all right. What did . . . Doctor Machelle tell you?"

"Enough," he answered laconically. He looked suddenly grim. "Why didn't you tell me about your mother instead of turning down my first proposal as if you didn't care?"

Laurel moistened dry lips. "But I did and do care enormously. Too much to tie you down to a wife who could never have been one while Mother was alive."

"So you shut me out."

"Could I have done anything else? Wouldn't you have done the same?"

He shrugged. "With me behind you you would have been better equipped to fight the undercurrents, whereas we've wasted so much time. And now it's. . . ." He broke off suddenly and her heart went cold.

Her overwhelming love for him urged her to throw herself into his arms and tell him how shattered she had been. But a sense of delicacy held her back. Laurel braced herself for what was coming.

Piteously, she held out her hands. "I . . . I did what I had to do. Kirk, I'm sorry."

He took the small hot quivering hands in his strong grasp, drew her in his arms and kissing her hair, let her go.

"You've had a bad time of it, my sweet. I hope I'm not rushing you." A finger beneath her rounded chin was compelling her to look at him. "Still want to marry me?"

Laurel's blue eyes searched his; she wished heartbreakingly that she knew the real reason behind the question. But his eyes remained enigmatic.

"I came all this way to marry you, Kirk," she answered soberly.

"So you did." He released her chin with a playful tweak. "And now suppose I show you around the hotel?"

"This hotel?" she queried in bewilderment.

"Of course." He was smiling now, that smile of extraordinary charm which did things to her heart. "We're getting married and the Japanese specialize in weddings. The New Otani is a rather special hotel where weddings are concerned."

Kirk escorted her down to the ground floor where Laurel saw not only banqueting halls but everything required for a wedding. The banqueting halls ranged from modest ones catering for a small party to enormous places spacious enough to cater for a thousand or so guests buffet fashion.

Everything the Western world could produce was there, from television to all kinds of electronic equipment. There were photographic studios, for wedding pictures, make-up rooms, dressing rooms and shops selling everything from wedding presents to wedding attire. A shop which interested Laurel hired out wedding clothes. Thus one could enter the hotel in a business suit, change to hired wedding attire for the ceremony and reception, then change back again before leaving the hotel.

Laurel learned that the Japanese wore a morning suit complete with carnation in their buttonhole for their wedding. She also fell in love with the bride's traditional white kimono with its elaborate trimmings and the beautifully coiffured wig lacquered to firmness and decorated with flowers.

"Do they marry in church?" she asked Kirk as they gazed at a splendid six-tier wedding cake in an illuminated alcove.

"They marry in the Shinto Wedding Ceremony Hall. Come on, I'll show you."

He led her into a beautifully decorated wood-panelled hall containing all the accoutrements for a Shinto wedding. A white-robed priest was already there and it was obvious that a wedding would soon be taking place.

From there they were taken to the kitchens by a supervisor who, on recognising Kirk, came forward to take them through. Bowing low from the waist, he had explained in English that the hotel kitchens were apart from those catering for weddings for which they employed a special staff. They were the last thing in efficiency and up-to-date equipment.

The reception after a Japanese wedding was much the same as the Western world with the exception of an orchestra which was hired even for the smallest gathering often on a smaller scale with fewer instuments.

"Well, what did you think about it?"

Kirk asked the question lazily, but his eyes were keen to see her reaction.

Laurel shone up at him. "I think it's fabulous. Shall . . . shall we be married here?"

"You don't mind?"

"I shall love it."

They had lunch in the Rose Room of the hotel where Kirk chose a Western-style meal.

"Enjoying it?" he asked when, having finished the meal, they were waiting for their coffee. He had lit a cigarette and was leaning back in his chair surveying her face mockingly.

"Very much," Laurel smiled. "It tastes different, but deliciously so."

He leaned forward to tap the ash from his cigarette on to an ash tray provided. "Amazing, isn't it? But I can see you're going to like Japan. You'll like the Japanese dishes. They have a certain gastronomic delicacy offering a new world of cuisine. I found it both adventurous and pleasing. I still do."

"Even raw fish?"

He grinned. "Yes, raw prawns, octopus, eel liver are extremely palatable."

The waiter brought their coffee. When he had gone, Laurel asked casually,

"Shall we have a place of our own or ... or shall I move in with you?"

"We have a place of our own which I'm keeping as a surprise – a new house which we shall move into when we return from our honeymoon." His eyes met hers suddenly and pierced her with their steeliness. "Are you looking forward to it, or are you worried?"

"I much prefer a place of our own, of course." She wanted to add that anywhere would be home with him, but found herself tonguetied. Besides, he was looking at her with a strange glitter in his eyes which affected her oddly.

"Afraid?" he mocked.

"Should I be? Perhaps I am a little."

He laughed softly as though at some secret joke. "I think we're going to be very happy. By the way, I'm not taking you to meet any of my friends yet. Time enough when we return from our honeymoon." He stubbed out his cigarette. "What would you like to do this afternoon?"

"I'd like to go around the shops," Laurel said, adding hurriedly at his raised eyebrows, "Not to buy, only to look."

"Why not to buy? I was hoping you would say that, because we have an important bit of shopping to do."

That afternoon strolling through narrow streets of shops with Kirk's hand clasping hers was something Laurel never forgot – the clip-clop of wooden clogs mingled with the high-pitched tinkling voices of vendors selling their wares in narrow streets closed to traffic where brightly coloured Japanese lanterns swung in the warm air alongside picturesque lanterns and English names over shops.

Shop fronts were open to the weather, displaying their wares with lantern-lit dim interiors like Aladdin's caves. Laurel would have liked a camera to take the scenes as they passed them by – the old fortune-teller in the dim recess of a shop leaning over a pretty kimonoed girl's hand beneath an orange lantern, the wizened old man roasting chestnuts over a brazier and the boy in a beautiful kimono of hand-painted birds and sunsets carrying a fairy temple of white wood rather like a Christmas tree with little drawers which opened out and contained sweets.

Now and then Kirk looked down on her enchanted glowing face with mocking amusement as she gazed on these delights, imprisoning them for all time in her heart. Occasionally, he drew her closer to his side when children and dogs dashed madly along the pavements as they will do in any country. Leisurely, they strolled by displays of household goods, market produce, flowers, fish, confectionery, rich silks, kimonos, jewellery, real pearls, Shinto shrines and little Buddhas carved in silver, jade and wood.

At a small jewellers, Kirk bought her a necklace, bracelet and ear-rings in jade and was highly amused when the little old shopkeeper with a face like a walnut presented her with a jade comb to wear in her hair.

Laurel was so touched by the gift that she felt tears welling

25

in her eyes.

"Honourable lady not like?"

The little walnut face with two very concerned shoe-button eyes regarded her pathetically.

"Oh yes! It's beautiful, and so kind of you." Laurel blinked back the tears as she groped for the appropriate Japanese words. "*Arigato gozaimasu.*"

She then bent forward to kiss the parchment-like cheek and looked up to see Kirk smiling at her mockingly.

"That old rascal was evidently smitten with you," he said when they were making their way back to the car. "I can see you being very popular with the males. You will find them very eager to please – only don't go round kissing them for doing you a favour!"

Kirk jealous? A delicious thought. Laurel hugged it to her, hoping it was true.

"He was a sweet old man, and quite harmless."

"I'm not so sure. The average Japanese male, apart from about thirty per cent, is very much a man, and don't forget it," he said dryly.

They had reached his car and he had opened the door for her to slip inside.

"I'll take your word for it," she said.

His lips twitched. "I wasn't aware that you could speak Japanese."

"Only the essentials for good manners," was the demure answer as she entered the car.

Their next place of call was a high-class establishment in the Imperial arcade. A young man in a black morning suit came forward to greet them, bowed his beautiful sleek black head and escorted them to a small private room where they were seated in ornate gilt chairs. He then proceeded to place trays of wedding rings on the glass counter before them Laurel's finger was measured, the correct size offered for Kirk to choose one, and he promptly slipped it on her finger.

"Comfortable?" he asked, highly amused at her flushed cheeks. She nodded. The wedding rings were withdrawn and trays of engagement rings winked at them.

"You choose, my sweet," Kirk said. "I'm sorry I couldn't send you one. I had no idea of your size."

Laurel leaned forward, wondering about their cost. That they were real diamonds, she had no doubt. She settled at last on a diamond solitaire. Kirk pushed it on her finger. His firm mouth tilted.

"I was about to choose that one myself. Do you like it?"

"It's beautiful," she assured him, smiling up into his grey gaze. Then while the young man whipped away the rings she drew his head down and kissed him on the lips. "Thank you."

"Tired?" Kirk was setting the car off at speed and they were leaving the shops behind.

"Of course not."

Laurel looked down at the engagement ring sparkling on her finger. Already she felt part of Kirk. How could she possibly be tired on such a singularly beautiful day, savouring the delights of being alone with him in exploring a beautifully strange new world? She already felt stronger and for the first time since her parents' tragic accident was carefree and happy. There was a breathless expectancy in the air too new to dwell upon, but it thrilled her all the same.

She found herself shining up at Kirk with joyful anticipation when he suggested taking her to a Buddhist temple for the tea ceremony.

"I think you'll enjoy it," he said.

He drove through open thoroughfares between streams of traffic until they reached a high stone wall enclosing many carved picturesque pagoda roofs. Leaving the car outside the gates, Kirk and Laurel entered the grounds. To Laurel it appeared to be a garden of temples and as they strolled past the first one, she had a glimpse of brass and gold shining in the dim interior.

The second beautifully carved unpainted wooden building had many pagoda roofs curling against the blue of the sky. The main entrance door was guarded by two stone dragons. At the top of the steps they slipped out of their shoes to put on the canvas slippers provided, then Kirk opened the door of an office-like room and guided Laurel inside.

Instantly, a beautifully painted paper door in the far wall was drawn along and a thin, ascetic-looking Japanese strode in wearing a long black lace robe over a white silk undergarment.

"The high priest," Kirk whispered to Laurel as he walked towards them. A thin strip of obi cloth in scarlet and gold was draped around his neck to hang down the front of his robes. His hair was cut in the manner of a monk and his yellow clean shaven face was wreathed in smiles.

"Kirk-san! How good to see you," he said in excellent English, bowing low.

Kirk introduced Laurel and after several more courteous bows the priest led them across the room to the painted paper sliding door. Along corridors and through a hall they went to yet another painted paper door.

At first the room they entered appeared to be empty except for the gold-edged tatami mats on the wooden floor. Then across an area of gloom Laurel saw an enormous golden Buddha with the usual large head, heavy hooded eyes and enigmatic expression. On each side of this awe-inspiring figure with its halo of golden flowers were beaten gold lotus flowers holding lighted candles.

The smell of incense burning stung Laurel's nostrils as her

eyes followed elaborate golden frescoes which leapt and twirled over the altar in the shape of flowers, lambs and saints. There were cabinets of treasures around the room, but the smell of incense was overpowering and Laurel was thankful to feel the comforting grip of Kirk's hand on her elbow as they left the room.

They walked with the priest through another long hall and through yet another paper sliding door. This opened on to a garden of miniature trees and lawns. Kneeling on cushions on the lawn were three young Japanese girls in kimonos facing an older woman in a black one.

"Enjoy your tea ceremony," said the priest smilingly as he motioned Kirk and Laurel to cushions by the girls on the grass then he left them.

Kirk folded his long legs with the ease of long practice. Laurel met his ironic gaze as she sat down gracefully beside him.

"The lady in black is teaching the girls the tea ceremony," he whispered. "It's one of the essentials in learning to be a good wife."

As he spoke one of the girls gave her attention to a kettle about to boil over a charcoal burner in front of her. Almost reverently, she poured a little of the water into a small porcelain bowl to heat it as one would heat a teapot. Then, beneath the eagle eye of the teacher, she measured out green powdered tea into the bowl. The boiling water was then poured over it and whisked around with a small bamboo-whiskered brush. Gravely the girl took the bowl in her left hand, turning it round slowly twice and gave it to Kirk.

He again turned it around twice before drinking it. The same procedure, making the tea in the small bowl and whisking it into a green froth, was gone through again, this time for Laurel. Carefully, she turned the bowl around twice and raised it to her lips. The slightly pungent flavour was delicious. So were the tiny jelly cakes served on toy plates.

The teacher watched the girl making every move with her dainty hands, nodding and smiling graciously at Kirk and Laurel as they received the tea. She spoke English fluently and conversed with them, keeping one eye on her pupil as she did so. Laurel enjoyed it all immensely.

That evening they dined out at the Fontainebleau restaurant on the top floor of the Imperial Hotel. It was expensive and elegant. Later, they walked in the gardens. It was a lovely evening with the silver sickle moon low in the wide expanse of sky. Earlier, they had looked down on the glitter of Tokyo by night, a mixture of the old and the new with modern neon lights nudging the centuries-old designed Japanese lanterns.

As she strolled beside Kirk along the gravel path, Laurel's heart began to beat painfully, not because they were hurrying but because he appeared to be strolling in the gardens with her for a purpose. Leisurely, they had passed over small bamboo bridges spanning rock pools until they reached a dainty pagoda-roofed pavilion where they paused at the top of the steps to admire the view.

They stood without contact but close enough for Laurel to wonder if he could hear the beating of her heart. Tremors ran along her nerves and she shivered.

He stood motionless for a second. Then he gripped her shoulders and turned her round to face him. "Are you cold?"

"No. Not in the least," she hastened to reassure him. "It's not a cold night, is it? Perhaps it's all the excitement of a strange country."

Her face was lifted very earnest and appealing to his and she saw him smile oddly.

"Are you sure that's all?" he asked softly. "You're not afraid of me, are you, Laurel?"

"Of course not." she grew suddenly rigid under his hands "Only I'm not the girl I was twelve months ago. I'm almost a stranger to you."

He said roughly, "We should have been married by now if you'd accepted my first proposal."

"I know. But I've been ill since then . . . and . . . Kirk, you're not marrying me because you feel sorry for me?" Her voice held the sound of tears.

"No, I'm not. I asked you to marry me for the usual reasons. Incidentally, I've never asked a woman to marry me before."

For a moment Laurel could have sworn the look in his eyes was one of regret. But it went as quick as it had appeared. Nevertheless she seemed to sense his sudden withdrawal. It was all wrong. She should be laughing up at him, telling him that she was a sacred idiot. With every fibre of her being she wanted this cool, lean arrogant man with his strength of character, the steady gaze of grey eyes beneath dark brows, his nonchalant grace of movement and his charm.

"You . . . you don't regret it, then? After all, twelve months apart is a long time."

"You're not trying to wriggle out of it, are you, my sweet? You know, you are afraid of me." The hands that held her arms closed with a steady pressure. "I know we've been apart for a while, but I promise you won't regret marrying me." His eyes twinkled down at her. "I promise not to beat you more than twice a week."

He had evaded her question. His reply had been too absolute to admit of any doubt on her part. If only he would follow up his teasing with taking her in his arms. Then she could have told him her fears. But he did not.

Laurel made a valiant attempt at humour. "That's what I call a very generous offer, Kirk-san."

"And you accept, my little lotus flower?"

31

He was smiling down at her with the smile that rocked her heart. He was so tall, so dear with his dark head silhouetted against the night sky. She wanted to put her arms around his neck and know the comforting warmth of his embrace.

Instead, she gave a heroic little smile. "Unreservedly," she answered.

Was the sudden intake of breath one of relief on his part or dismay? Laurel wished she could stop torturing herself as he took her hand.

"Come on, sit down. I want to talk to you."

He led her inside the pavilion and she sank down on the wooden seat. He did not sit down beside her but stood leaning against the door frame showing her his rather stern profile as he gazed out into the night.

"I had intended us getting married immediately you arrived. However, on second thoughts I decided that it wouldn't be fair to you after an exhausting journey, especially as you were recuperating from a run-down condition."

"I'm much better. Doctor Machelle said I would soon pick up again."

"Undoubtedly. You're young and resilient. But you've had a rough time. We must get you well, and that means no extra exertion until you can take it in your stride."

"I've never been ill in my life before. . . ."

"I know," he cut in somewhat impatiently. "You're the kind of little idiot that would keep on until you dropped."

"But I'm well now, honestly, Kirk."

"Are you?" Without having moved he was bending over her in one swoop, looking down at her in the gloom with an expression that stirred her pulses alarmingly. "Are you?" he repeated. "Well enough to marry me this coming Saturday?"

Laurel's heart lurched near her throat. "This . . . this coming Saturday?" she echoed weakly.

"That's what I said." He frowned. "Is it too soon? Do you feel I'm rushing you?"

"No."

He straightened but he did not smile. "We won't discuss it now. You've done enough for one day. I'll make all the arrangements. And you're not to worry. I'm taking time off for the rest of the week to show you around – unless you'd rather rest until Saturday?"

"No." Laurel rose to her feet to put a hand on his sleeve. "I'm not an invalid, Kirk. I never have been."

His frown disappeared and he gave a semblance of a smile. "Even so, there'll be no late nights for you, my sweet, for a long time to come."

CHAPTER THREE

KIRK was careful not to subject Laurel to any degree of strain, during the next few days and she was so happy to be with him that the time simply flew. He took her out to dine most evenings, sometimes in an expensive plush restaurant like Maxim's in the Gintza, a replica of Maxim's in Paris with French cusine and the old-world atmosphere. Other times they went to an inn to dine Japanese-style or to one of the many night spots where they could dance in between courses in the warm intimacy of shaded lights.

Their days were spent leisurely in the parks or in the country where they picnicked with a basket made up at the hotel. And each day Laurel became more and more enchanted with the fragile and delicate charm of a strange and beautiful country. She loved the dainty snow-covered peaks piercing the blue skies, the beautiful willow pattern gardens, the little yellow people in their mushroom hats patiently wading in the mud of their rice paddies to plant the delicate green shoots, and hardworking mothers carrying their fat little babies strapped to their backs and the round bland, smiling faces of the shopkeepers frankly admitting their pleasure to be of service.

Looking back afterwards on those few days with Kirk, Laurel realized that she was beginning to recover her former health and strength, to pick up the threads of life again which the tragedy of her parents had unravelled.

Saturday morning dawned with Laurel waking up to her wedding day. She was up early for breakfast in order to go downstairs to the hairdressing salon. Keeping her mind a careful blank, she put on the black silk trouser suit, found it impossible to eat a thing and drank several cups of coffee.

Her appointment had been booked and she was greeted by the proprietor, a small gold-toothed young man who bowed her ceremoniously to a chair in one of the cubicles in the salon. In excellent English, he complimented her on her beautiful hair as he dressed it up expertly. The salon was filled with clients and Laurel wondered how many brides there were among them. Her pulses were making themselves felt despite her outer calm and she was thankful her hairdresser was not a chatty female who would want to discuss her wedding.

Last-minute jitters – that was what she had got. Had Kirk got them too? She doubted it, although, like herself, he would be glad when it was over. The thoughts ended as the proprietor excused himself to answer a personal call on the phone and Laurel's wits were sharpened when she heard Kirk's name mentioned by a voice coming clearly through the paper-thin wall of the next cubicle.

The first voice was saying,

"I'm surprised he hasn't introduced his future wife to his friends."

"Who, Kirk? She's probably in this very hotel. It seems he's kept her out of the way. No one knows where she's staying."

"I asked Bill to find out something about her when he went to the stag party Kirk gave last night at the club," said the first voice.

"And did he?"

"No. I believe Kirk was as close as an oyster and refused to be drawn. By the way, Kirk wouldn't get to bed before four this morning. It was getting on for four when Bill came home and Kirk was still there."

"Well, there won't be anything bleary-eyed about Kirk at his wedding. He's so full of health and vitality that one late night won't make much difference to him." The second voice was cynical for a woman. "Dennis came home blotto and he'll have bags under his eyes all day to prove it. I wish he had a bit of Kirk's strength of character."

The first voice heaved a sigh. "Bill wasn't too bad. Do you know, I'm sorry Kirk is getting married. He's such a good sport. And all the women had their eye on him, even the married ones. I bet his wife will be one of those jealous possessive creatures who'll watch him like a hawk."

"If she is it won't take her long to keep a certain female at bay."

"You mean Countess Nina?"

"Who else? She's regarded Kirk as her property for long enough. I shall enjoy seeing someone put her in her place. You don't think Kirk is marrying for a blind, do you? I mean, Nina has been very obvious in her preference for his company of late. Kirk might be starting as he means to go on and keep his wife in the background, so to speak. Maybe she isn't the possessive kind. She's probably docile and will turn a blind eye to Kirk's friendship with Nina."

"Do you think so? You could be right. I could imagine a girl being glad of having Kirk on any terms. He's so exciting, so everything. Not feeling jealous, are you, Jean?"

Jean's laugh grated. "Maybe I am at that. I'm ready to bet that she's starry-eyed and so blindly in love that she can't see where she's going. I know because I was the same. Look where it got me."

"Well, you would go in for looks. You should have gone in for a beanpole with a face like a bad ham and been gloriously happy like me with my Bill."

"Well, the girl has certainly done well for herself. Everyone knows that Kirk is on the way up – the Emperor will see to

36

that. He's very fond of him."

"I wonder if he's told His Nibs he's getting married. Funny he should decide to get married when he's away."

"Yes, it's all so hush-hush, isn't it? Kirk's taken no leave either for twelve months apart from that little business trip to Honolulu when he came back with that millionaire and his two pretty daughters. I'm surprised Kirk didn't marry one of them. They were crazy about him."

"He could be saving his leave for a long honeymoon. This girl he's marrying is English, isn't she?"

"As far as we know. Well, it won't be long before we see what she's like. I'm terribly disappointed we couldn't get the boss to do our hair. Apparently he's with some important client."

Laurel took this to mean herself. She longed to be able to see the speakers who had inadvertently pricked her bubble of happiness. She was remembering Kirk's bitterness about her refusing his first proposal of marriage. Had he wanted to tell her then that he had found someone else who was more his kind? Countess Nina, beautiful, rich and influential. Laurel felt the perspiration of doubt on her temples. The perfumed salon suddenly became overpowering, unbearable.

Then the proprietor was back, apologizing profusely for the delay. He picked up the comb and his deft fingers plaited the dark locks of hair into a thing of beauty. Laurel recovered her composure enough to smile when he held the jade mirror at the back of her head to show her the result of his labours. She showed the correct degree of enthusiasm and marvelled that she could be so calm outwardly when she was trembling within.

Taking off the protective cape from her slim shoulders, he brushed off all imaginary hairs from her suit and retreated in horror when she offered to pay for the service.

"No. Kirk-san very good friend. Honoured to do honourable lady's hair."

Laurel pleaded, "Please take something."

But he was adamant. "Happy to be of service. Wish honourable lady much happiness and many children."

The gold teeth flashed as he bowed her out. On her way back to her room Laurel was a prey to tormented thoughts hammering unceasingly in her head, stealing the colour from her cheeks, the light from her eyes and the buoyancy from her step. The menacing cloud that had descended after the tragic accident to her parents had never really lifted. The two voices she had heard were only a part of it. Had Kirk really hoped she would change her mind?

Was it the reason Kirk had not introduced her to his friends? Laurel was too pure-minded to see double-dealing in others and she was sure Kirk would not resort to it. But he was in the Diplomatic Service and was trained in such matters. During the trying time with her mother, Laurel had not been fully aware of the extent to which he had filled her life. She had cared desperately for him all along. Yet it was not until she had seen him again that her love for him had leapt into flame, a flame which she could not quench.

In vain, Laurel told herself to have it out with him and give him back his ring if he did not wish to marry her. She lifted a hand to her throbbing temples. It would be impossible to tear him out of her heart without dying a little. Feverishly, recalling a touch, a certain tone in his voice, she could have sworn he loved her. Then calm reason whispered – he had hardly behaved like a lover. There had been the cool kiss on the ship and the rather cruel one on her first morning at the hotel when he had brought her the flowers. After that, what? A cool kiss on her hair when he left her at the door of her hotel room.

Laurel's sensitive nature trembled at the thought of giving her love where it was not wanted. Her face burned with shame at the thought. Tears pricked her eyes as she closed the door of her room and leaned back against it. How weak we are when put to the test, she thought bitterly. One of the women in the hairdressing salon had said that a girl would be happy to take Kirk on any terms. Was she so devoid of pride as to be that kind of person?

If only she had time to think! But the sudden tap on the door behind her told her she had not even got that. It sounded like the crack of doom.

With a groping movement Laurel found the catch of the door and opened it. A young woman stood there holding the bouquet. She was wearing a very pretty kimono in turquoise. Laurel warmed to the bright smile on her little yellow moon face.

"Your flowers, honourable lady," she said in soft perfect English. "I, Mini-san, have come to help you prepare for wedding."

Laurel stepped aside to allow her to enter. First came the exquisite lace and satin bra, panties and matching underskirt. Then the dress, which zipped up her slim back, emphasizing her small firm bust deliciously. The tiny stand-up collar gave her a demure touch of dignity and the long wide sleeves added an elegant finish to a beautifully modelled dress which fitted her willowy figure to perfection.

"Honourable lady have skin like peaches and cream. Pale now like bride. Japanese bride have whitened face. It is traditional." She peeped over Laurel's shoulder as she sat before the dressing table mirror. "Not much make-up needed."

Mini-san then proceeded to touch up Laurel's eyelashes. The tiny hands enchanted Laurel as they carried out their task, ending with the tiny coronet of flowers being placed on top of the beautifully coiffured hair to hold the long veil in position.

39

"Bride beautiful like angel," Mini-san cooed when Laurel was ready.

But no little bluebird of happiness sang in Laurel's cold heart when she surveyed her own enchanting apparition in the mirror. All feeling seemed to have deserted her as she took the bouquet that Mini-san offered.

She wondered if Kirk would be waiting for her downstairs or if he would change his mind and slide out of it at the last moment. But no note came and she went downstairs with Mini-san beside her. At the entrance to the wedding hall stood a very good-looking Japanese in morning suit with a carnation in his buttonhole and beside him stood two delightful tots dressed as bridesmaids. Around five years old, they were as alike as two peas in a pod in white organza with two frilly little caps on their black pageboy-styled heads. They looked so delicious with their pretty almond-shaped eyes and rosebud mouths that Laurel could have picked them up and hugged them.

When Mini-san introduced them they bowed almost to the floor. They were named Ranko (Little Orchid) and Mariko (Little Ball). The New Atani Hotel certainly had everything laid on, Laurel thought a little hysterically, and was torn between laughter and tears.

The good-looking Japanese was introduced as Kasuti-san, a colleague of Kirk. He was to give her away. They entered on cue to soft music, Laurel with her hand on the black sleeve of Kasuti-san. Kirk was waiting for her with a man in the uniform of a captain in the British Navy. She learned later that his ship was in Yokohama for repairs and that he was an old school friend of Kirk's.

As she moved to join him a startled flicker of appraisal appeared in his clear grey eyes. Then it was gone. He took her cold hand firmly in his warm one and Laurel gave herself to him

40

for all time. The English ceremony was brief, after which Laurel was introduced to a blur of faces.

Photographs were taken and soon they were sitting in the centre of a long elaborately set table facing a three-tier wedding cake in one of the banqueting rooms. A horde of congratulatory telegrams were read, including one from Kirk's Uncle George, by the best man, the wedding cake was cut with Kirk's firm steady hand over Laurel's shaky one and he made a sparkling speech.

Later, Laurel had gone upstairs to change with the help of Mini-san and it was all over.

"Not too bad, was it?"

Kirk was pushing the long opulent car at speed on the first stage of their honeymoon. He looked careless and debonair in a light grey lounge suit while Laurel sat beside him gazing through the windscreen with a pale set face.

It was a day of soft sunshine and gay enchanting shade. But Kirk was intent upon speed and the scenery swept by like pictures on a screen. To Laurel the wedding had been one of real beauty – the tiny bridesmaids, the beautifully decorated room filled with enchanting flower arrangements which had continued into the banqueting room, the gay kimonos mingling with the European dress of the guests and the soft classical music from an orchestra, a splendid background for all the courtesy.

She said wistfully, "I thought it was rather lovely. The Japanese are unique in the way they have of putting beauty before everything."

He said carelessly, "I knew you would enjoy it. I know every woman dreams of a wedding with all the trimmings and the photographs to drool over afterwards. I didn't want to deprive you of it. For myself I would have preferred something short and sweet."

Laurel eyed him covertly. He looked strong, lean and unshakeable, his grey eyes beneath straight black brows, steady and cool. If only he would look at her like a lover or stop the car and kiss her! It would be only too easy then to tell him of her fears. But he did neither. He merely presented a dark profile which caught painfully at her heart-strings.

Even if the wedding should turn out to be a mockery, she had to hand it to him for the superb handling of it.

"Thanks for everything you've done, Kirk," she said. "For giving me the wedding every woman dreams of. It's something I shall never forget, especially since, like a man, you wanted no fuss. Are you glad it's over?"

He tossed her a questioning glance. "Are you?"

Again the evasion, she thought. "I suppose so."

During the journey to Japan, Laurel had looked upon her marriage as glorifying everything by its radiance, lifting her to the heights of happiness and ecstasy. Instead, all she felt was a strange unhappy bewilderment, an anguished doubt emphasized by the torture of his nearness. Here they were sitting side by side yet kept miles apart by some strange undercurrent against which she was powerless to resist. Perhaps, she thought drearily, she was too feeble to deal with the unseen barrier which seemed more formidable when they were alone.

The house in which they were to spend their honeymoon was at Kamakura Bay, a little town of historic interest about thirty miles or so from Tokyo. The big car ate up the miles of pot-holed roads with an easy assurance, tossing aside little hamlets of brown wooden houses and Japanese inns enclosed by cherry orchards heavy with blossom.

Wealthy friends of Kirk had offered the house which they used mostly as a holiday home. It was situated on the side of a mountain overlooking the bay. Kirk had driven with considerable dexterity along bumpy roads with rolling seas of rice on either side thinning out to hills that gave glimpses of beaches caressed by shimmers of blue water. A magnificent stone Buddha looked down from a hill top as hills became mountains and tea marched with rice up the sides.

A road lined with Japanese cedars veered upwards and several curving country roads brought them eventually to the gates of the house. They were evidently expected, for the gates were open to receive them. Laurel saw a Japanese garden of miniature trees, enchanting small rustic bamboo bridges over streams with flowers and stone lanterns placed with Japanese artistry on sloping lawns.

The house, built of carved wood, rose mellow and serene in the sun like a showpiece in a garden setting. A young man in a white jacket over black trousers stood in the doorway. His jet black hair was brushed back from a sallow face to which only his eyes gave colour. They were a perfect almond shape and twinkled as he bowed low from the waist to greet them.

Kirk had helped Laurel from the car. "Darling," he said, "this is Yuseku-san who'll look after us while we are here."

Yuseku-san bowed low again greeting Laurel in perfect English before fetching the luggage from the car.

"Tired, my sweet?"

Kirk swept her up into his arms to carry her over the threshold, then set her down in the tiny vestibule between the two front doors. Here they faced a row of house slippers, and kneeling down, Kirk took off her shoes to choose her small size from those provided and put them on her feet.

"I'm not in the least tired," she answered as he discarded his own footwear in favour of the slippers. "Please can I see over the house? It looks delightful."

Laurel was surprised at the spaciousness of the rooms where sunlight fell slantingly through tall windows on to elegant furniture and highly polished wooden floors. Crystal chandeliers

43

winked, a lacquer cabinet gleamed with objets d'art, a gold Buddha on an ebony pedestal looked mysteriously mellow and flowers were everywhere in jade bowls and beautiful vases.

The house was unusual. Half the rooms were furnished in Western style. The rest, in Japanese, would not concern them since Kirk did not intend them entertaining visitors on their honeymoon. It was evident that no expense had been spared on furnishing the house, and Laurel walked through it wide-eyed.

"It's awfully grand, Kirk. Are your friends so wealthy?" she asked as they entered the main bedroom.

"So-so," was the laconic reply. His mouth twitched with amusement as she looked anywhere but at the bed. "This is to be our suite of rooms. I have a dressing room leading off." He inclined his head towards a communicating door. "I'm going to wash and change for dinner. Take your time, there's no hurry."

Laurel walked to the window to see the view across the sea, which delighted her immensely. She imagined them going down to the little secluded beach just visible below a winding path. There was a white curve of foam where the water washed gently on the shore. They would bathe together and get to know each other again. All her fears had been groundless, purely pre-wedding nerves. It was a big thing to give oneself unreservedly into someone else's keeping, especially someone like Kirk whom she knew so little about. But it was going to be heaven, Laurel told herself as she swung round to look at the room she was to share with him.

The fourposter bed dominated the room with diaphanous drapes cascading down from the canopy overhead framing the cluster of cushions placed artistically at the bedhead. Rich dark furniture and a scarlet-fringed bedside lamp looked dramatic against neutral walls. The whole effect was one of warm enveloping sumptuousness.

44

Lightheartedly, Laurel unpacked her cases brought in by Yuseku-san, filling available space with her pretty trousseau and placing her frothy nightdress of ribbons and lace on the bed. The last thing in her case was the leather case of masculine brushes, her wedding present to Kirk. She looked down at it thoughtfully for a moment and on a sudden impulse she crossed the room to the communicating door.

Opening it quietly, she crept into the empty room. Yuseku had obviously unpacked Kirk's clothes, as his cases were no-where to be seen in this masculine room which contained a bed, dressing table, wardrobe, writing desk and two comfort-able chairs. Kirk was in the bathroom, for she could hear the water running and somewhat disappointed not to find him there, Laurel put the case down on the dressing table. As she did so she saw his pyjamas folded neatly on the bed.

Laurel frowned, wondering why they should be there. Then it occurred to her that Yuseku-san had laid them out for Kirk to undress that evening in his dressing room. The incident was forgotten as Laurel returned to her room to wash and dress for dinner. She took care to keep her hair immaculate in the process and blessed her frock for zipping all down the back to enable her to step into it. After she had made up her face light-ly the result in the mirror was pleasing. The long fluid lines of the dress in a soft shade of rose accentuated her slimness and she was considering whether to put on the jade necklace to fill the scooped-up neckline when Kirk strode in.

The next moment something cold was clasped around her neck and she saw the fire of diamonds as Kirk lowered his head to look over her shoulder into the mirror. He smelled of cedar-wood soap and his tanned face was like bronze beside her pale one. His cool lips brushed her cheek.

"Thanks for the brushes, my sweet. I hope you like your present."

Laurel fingered the diamonds. "But, Kirk, they look real. I ... I'll be scared of losing them."

He turned her round to face him, taking his time at looking her over, taking in the slender youthful curves of her figure before concentrating on the braids of rich dark hair.

"Well, well, Mrs. Graham," he said softly. "You're full of surprises. This morning you were an angel in bridal array, now you're a dusky beauty in rose pink who can't be real. Or are you?" He bent his head as though drawn against his will to seek her mouth. Suddenly, he straightened and laughed. "You're looking far too lovely for my peace of mind. Come on, we'd better go in to dinner or Yuseku-san will be wondering what's keeping us."

The dinner was proof of Yuseku-san's skill as a chef. Kirk provided most of the conversation by talking about Japan. They went into the lounge for coffee and while Yuseku served it, Kirk put a long-playing record on the radiogram.

They sat together on the settee and Kirk took a cigarette case from his pocket.

"Cigarette?"

"Not now, thanks," she said. Then hoping he would not think her too unsophisticated, she added hurriedly, "I do smoke sometimes, but not very often. In fact, I don't really enjoy it."

He lighted one for himself, blew a line of smoke in the air and said disarmingly, "Don't be apologetic about it. I'm glad – I hate a woman to reek of tobacco smoke. Come here."

He put out a long arm and scooped her up beside him, drawing her head back on his chest. The soft music that really was music and not a blaring noise, washed over them. Laurel closed her eyes. Doubt and misgiving drifted away. She was here with Kirk and nothing else mattered.

The next thing she knew was his firm mouth resting briefly

on her own.

She opened her eyes sleepily to find his very close. "Oh dear, have I been asleep?" she said confusedly.

"For a little matter of two hours," he replied dryly. "What about a little stroll in the garden before bed?" He put her back against the settee and rose lazily to his feet. "I'll fetch your wrap. Take your time about wakening."

He was back in no time with a jacket which he slipped on her shoulders as she stood up. Then he drew her hand through his arm and they strolled out into the garden. Everything was so wonderful in the dusk of a Japanese night. The sky was a transparent sapphire, against which the branches of trees drooped like dark shapes cut from black paper. Overhead the moon looked down on silhouettes of fishing boats on the calm waters way out to sea and on the horizon a big Orient liner showed a necklace of light along her length.

Laurel's dress billowed lightly out as if she was indeed borne on the air, as they stood at the little wicket gate leading down to the beach. With her hand tucked in Kirk's arm she was filled with a lightness of spirit, a kind of dreamlike ecstasy.

"The sea is as smooth as cream," she said.

"What about a sail? There's a boat waiting for us down at the jetty."

She shone up at him. "Could we? I'd love it."

"Come on, then."

He took her hand in his and they went down the path to the jetty where the boat was moored. Then they were on the water and Kirk was grinning down at her from the controls. He was all fire and laughter, his teeth gleaming in his dark face, his wide shoulders bracing up to the speed as he sent the boat leaping through the water like a porpoise.

As for Laurel, she shrank back deliciously from the onslaught of spray which took her breath away. Then she was holding up

47

her face, enjoying the tingling sensation on her skin. Returning to the shore was like falling from the heights on to the ordinary plain.

They returned to the lounge for a nightcap before going to bed. Kirk had rung Yuseku-san for fresh ice as he poured the drinks. Laurel wandered around the room admiring a lacquer cabinet filled with Japanese dolls in traditional dress before stopping at a portrait on the baby grand piano.

It was the head and shoulders of a beautiful woman in her twenties. Her face, with its high cheekbones, slanting eyes and pretty nose and mouth, was openly provocative. She held a fan just below her chin and there was a flower in the beautifully coiffured hair piled Japanese-fashion on her head. A Geisha girl, Laurel thought, or the wife of the owner of the house.

She sauntered to the chair Kirk was standing by with her drink and sank down in it, accepting the glass. Kirk did not sit down but stood indolently against the wall by the drinks cabinet.

"To us," he said, lifting his glass. "May all our troubles be little ones."

On a wave of shyness, Laurel lifted her glass, lowering her eyes from the gleam in his which filled her with a wonderful trembling joy. When he was like this at his most charming she had neither the will nor the desire to resist him. Her face grew hot, staining her cheeks to a wild rose. Her lips trembled in a smile.

"To us," she murmured, then before she could stop the words, they were spoken. "Who is she?"

"Who?" lazily.

"The lady in the portrait on the piano."

"Oh, that?" carelessly. "The lady of the house."

"You haven't told me anything about them. I suppose you've

been here before?"

"Many times."

"Are they Japanese?"

"Yes – Isohi and Nina Wanaka. To give them their correct title, the Count and Countess Wanaka."

A blast of cold wind swept Laurel from head to toe. The identity of the woman in the photograph smiling on them so mockingly came as a shock.

She took down part of her drink and marvelled at her steady hand as she looked towards the photograph.

"She's very lovely," she said inanely.

"Isn't she?"

Laurel gazed down into her glass – anywhere but at Kirk. "I don't remember seeing them at the wedding."

He did not answer for a moment and she raised her head to find him looking down at her enigmatically.

"They're away at the springs of Noboribetsu. It's a famous spa on the island of Hokkaido and a favourite resort with Tokyo residents. I'll take you there some time. You'll enjoy it."

Bitterly, Laurel told herself she must be unique as a bride who was spending her honeymoon in the house of her husband's girl-friend – or was it mistress? Tears choked her throat as she recalled the two voices in the hairdressing salon that morning. There was never any smoke without fire and if the two gossiping women were romancing a little there must be some truth in what they said. This Nina person was beautiful enough anyway to turn any man's head, even Kirk's.

Why then had he married Laurel? Because his lady love was unattainable, or to stop the gossiping tongues until the woman was free? The colour ebbed from her cheeks, leaving her face strangely white, her nerves were on wires pulling so tightly that they threatened to snap. She put the glass down on the low lacquer table. The walls of the room seemed to be closing in on her and she heard Kirk's voice coming from a great distance.

"Are you all right, Laurel? You look as pale as a ghost." He was bending over her after putting his glass down beside hers on the table. His keen grey eyes were raking hers with concern as he took her trembling hands in his.

She said, "Yes."

He held her hands gently. "Poor child! It's been a long and trying day for you. Come, I'm going to carry you to bed."

Before he could carry out his intention, Laurel was on her feet.

"Please, Kirk. I'm not an invalid, so don't treat me as one." How could he know that she did not want him near her at that moment? She was still trembling a little, but she had regained her self-control.

His hands gripped her then and he looked at her oddly. "My dear girl, you're my wife and I intend to look after you. Come along to bed. You'll feel better in the morning."

Kirk held her arm in a deceptively light hold and she walked with him to her room, too weary to protest. At her door she drew away from his hand. He opened it and followed her into the room.

"I'm all right now, thanks," she told him, her eyes straying to the fourposter bed. His pyjamas were not there. In that moment all feeling in her died. His hand came under her chin and she felt the coolness of his firm lips resting lightly on her own. He felt her tremble and there was no response.

His hand dropped. "Goodnight, my sweet. Sleep well."

Then he was gone into the adjoining room where he had intended sleeping all along. Laurel stood in the centre of the room trying to gather her confused thoughts into some kind of order to review the situation soberly.

Her head was woolly and her heart ached, but she willed

herself to see things in their true perspective. She was a bride, yet not a bride, a simple naïve girl who had fallen headlong in love with an experienced man of the world without knowing the least thing about his life. One thing was clear – she loved him irrevocably and completely. If he wanted her she was his for the taking, but he did not.

Laurel sank down upon the bed in despair. This Countess Nina had probably held him in her toils long before he had met herself. Even if the woman had only known Kirk recently that provocative smiling mouth and all that coquetry derived from experience was enough to persuade any man to forget even honour in his desire for her.

Laurel's soft mouth tightened stubbornly. One thing is certain, she thought, I'm not afraid of the woman and I don't care if she has had a head start. I've already burned my boats by marrying Kirk, but it won't stop me from building a new one. I love him far too much to make him a laughing stock in front of his friends by leaving him now. Besides, isn't that what Countess Nina wanted?

She shuddered to think how much she had changed in the last twenty-four hours. For instance, taking it for granted that the woman was no good. That she of all people who had always loved her fellow beings should harbour resentment and hatred against a complete stranger! It filled her with shame.

Granted, she was up against a woman who held all the winning cards. Nevertheless, she was a fast learner herself. The challenge roused all her old fighting spirit, feeble at the moment because her vitality had been drained by all the events of the past year. It was there, though, responding valiantly to her need.

Calmly, Laurel went over her weapons, beginning with her clothes. Her trousseau was pretty and feminine enough, though everything she bought from now on would have to be just that little bit more alluring. The flowered black silk trouser suit, for instance, did something to her pale skin and slim figure.

Wearily, she lifted a hand to her coiffured hair, surprised to find it had withstood the breeze on the sea. The silken tresses tumbled down, hardened by the lacquer used to keep them in place. That was going to be washed out for a start. Kirk disliked women to smoke and she was sure he preferred her hair to be soft and caressing with its own natural perfume.

Laurel wished she knew more about his likes and dislikes. The effort to please would be worth it for one warm husband's glance from those grey eyes. Deciding upon a line of action lifted her spirits and she felt almost lighthearted when she made her way to the bathroom.

CHAPTER FOUR

LAUREL awoke bemused with sleep to look around the strange room in brief bewilderment. Memory came flooding back and she looked at the little travelling clock on her bedside table. Eight o'clock. The house was silent above the soft swish of the waves washing against the beach below.

Her head, like the new wedding ring on her finger, felt as heavy as lead. No sound of movement from the adjoining room reached her ears as she slipped into a frothy negligée and went to the window. The garden, sloping down to the sea, brightened here and there by clouds of cherry blossom and lordly pines with red-gold branches, was backed by the serene lines of hills closing in on the scene like an old Japaense print. The beauty of the place struck Laurel as ironic — a veritable Eden which was owned by the serpent.

Laurel went towards the wardrobe to pick out something to wear. She had no idea of Kirk's plans for the day. He was probably up by the crack of dawn, out riding or swimming. At the moment her feelings were too slack for either. Exhilarating moments beneath the shower worked wonders and her step was buoyant when she peered into the adjoining room.

Kirk's bed was immaculate. There was no sign of him or Yuseku-san. No one in the dining room either. Laurel walked down the short passage to the door opening on to the kitchen garden. She was putting on the wooden garden shoes when Yuseku-san came in with lettuce from the garden. His round yellow face creased in a delighted smile as he answered

Laurel's "*Oheyo*," with a spate of tinkling English which she gathered was all about the weather and that he hoped she had slept well.

She said, "*Hoi. Arigato.*"

Two little words meaning, yes, thank you. The *Hoi* was spoken as *Hi*, which Laurel thought sounded gay. Her knowledge of the language was practically nil and she was discovering that smiles and gestures did very well for little things. Moreover, these small people with their crinkling laughing faces were so friendly that one never felt embarrassed when unable to find the right words. They seemed anxious only for her to understand their good will. The rest did not matter.

Laurel was clip-clopping along the garden path when a little brown mouse of a woman arrived obviously to do the chores. She wore a brown kimono and reminded Laurel of a wooden doll with her black pageboy-styled hair and mobile smile lighting up behind spectacles glinting in the sun. On seeing Laurel, she stopped, bowed low from the waist, giggled and hastened indoors.

Amused, Laurel continued along the garden path. Two gardeners were at work, clad in neat blue cotton trousers and jacket with *getas* on their feet. They smiled and bowed low as she passed on her way down towards the beach.

Kirk met her half way, a tall wide-shouldered figure in a bathrobe. A towel was flung carelessly over one shoulder and his tousled hair fell on his forehead in boyish tendrils. How extraordinarily attractive and arresting he was, she thought with a painful lurch of her heart. He was so intesely alive with a vitality and fire burning beneath the surface, a quality that excited and challenged.

"Hello there!" He put an arm around her shoulders, smiling down at her as they walked back to the house. "Slept well?" When she nodded, he went on, "I've been for a dip in the sea.

54

I looked in to ask you to come with me, but you were fast asleep. I accepted a loan of this house thinking it would give you the opportunity to relax. A hotel isn't the same. You have to quit your room after breakfast. Here, you can rest all day if you feel inclined."

You can also use two bedrooms without inviting the curiosity of a hotel staff, Laurel thought bitterly. The next moment she was regretting her bitterness, and smiled up at him sweetly in consequence.

"You're very kind," she said wisfully.

"And you're very sweet," he said, hugging her shoulders.

Laurel ought to have felt blissfully happy at that moment with Kirk's arm around her shoulders, but she wasn't. He hugged her like he would a pal. There was no way of discovering what he thought and what he intended to do about their marriage. It could not go on indefinitely as it was.

Even so, breakfast with Kirk sent her spirits soaring. He gave her his whole attention, ignoring the morning papers which Yuseku had placed beside him on the table. In between seeing that she made a good breakfast, he told her amusing incidents that had happened during his work at the Embassy. Gradually all strain and embarrassment left her as she responded to his teasing.

"How much Japanese do you know?"

Breakfast was over and Kirk was leaning back in his chair, having lighted a cigarette. Laurel watched the well kept hands, the lean brown fingers curling around the cigarette as he sent a spiral of smoke ceilingwards.

"Apart from his usual greetings, very little."

His mouth twitched. "Define very little."

"I know that *haro* means hello, *sekken* means soap, *orfuro* means bath and *miza*, water."

He regarded her with tolerant amusement. "My poor

sweet," he teased, "you were evidently determined to keep clean! You'll learn as you go along. Japanese is much easier to speak than to write. There's certainly nothing for you to worry about. The average Japanese male, like any other, has an eye for a pretty girl and he'll fall over himself to help you." He leaned forward to tap the ash from his cigarette into an ashtray provided on the low table. "However, you'll be with me most of the time."

He had leaned back again in his chair and Laurel looked up. His expression was quizzical and disturbingly direct. She was growing accustomed to his way of looking anyone straight in the eye. It was easy for him since he was so good at an enigmatic expression.

Laurel knew she was utterly transparent in her emotions and felt, as now, that Kirk could look through her like a clear pane of glass. Was she a fool to distrust his feeling for her, to be afraid to reach out for her own happiness? She could do it, lure him on and set the match to the flame of his passion. But she did not want him on those terms. He had to come to her with an agonizing love and need. He had to feel for her exactly how she felt about him. That was what marriage was all about.

She found refuge from the ensuing silence in speech. "Talking about Japanese males, I haven't yet seen any of those terrifically huge fat men who wrestle on the television."

"The Japanese call it Sumo, one of the oldest of sports. The men who take part are Japanese who go in for this kind of thing if they happen to be tall and husky as youngsters. They deliberately fatten themselves up through the years and do special exercises to develop their muscles. The minimum weight is a good two hundred and fifty pounds. Anything less and he would look thin and puny in the ring. Some of them are a colossal weight, which adds to the entertainment when in the ring. There are tournaments lasting about a fortnight in Tokyo, and there's one in May if you care to see it?"

Laurel shivered. "No, thank you!"

He teased. "Wouldn't you like to go just once just to see what it's like?" He was laughing at her revulsion. "Women do go. And they enjoy it."

"I'll take your word for it. Why do they wear their hair in a funny topknot?"

"It isn't a wig but their own hair allowed to grow long for the purpose of wearing it in the old feudal style of the Daimio or old feudal war-lords." He laughed at her mockingly with a devilish gleam in his eye as he added, "Their costume, a kind of loincloth, is supported solely by a belt." His chuckle was deliberate. "Now you're blushing."

"You meant me to."

"You do it so beautifully. I shall probably do it often." He leaned forward to stub out his cigarette. "You haven't much colour since your illness. I suggest we go out in the car this morning and spend the afternoon on the beach. It's sheltered and gets really hot in the sun. We can take the morning papers with us. If there are any magazines or books you'd like I'll order them for you."

Seated beside him in the big roomy car, Laurel felt happy and relaxed. The day was delightfully warm and sunny with Kirk suddenly much closer than he had been.

"My friends are a mixture of English and Japanese," he told her as they sped through villages of unpainted houses, shops and the usual Buddhist and Shinto shrines. "You'll like them."

Laurel thought of the two English voices she had heard in the hairdressing salon on her wedding morning. If only she had not heard them! Then their marriage would have had a better start. The strangeness of a foreign country seen through the eyes of a happy bride would have been far different, more bearable. Not that she felt alien. She did not. On the contrary, she felt at home. The small doll-like unpainted houses caught at her heart strings and the way the bright-eyed, hardworking little people smiled on their own humdrum existence made her feel ashamed when she had so much more. They passed farms and orchards where the fruit was protected from the birds by being covered in small bags, each one wrapped religiously, looking strangely like artificial trees. In the paddy fields whole families were working furiously and dedicatingly planting the shoots of their staple diet.

Kirk said, "We had a fortnight of rain before you arrived, a godsend to rice growers. After the negligent growth of a hard winter the spring rain sent up the rice shoots which are now ready for transplanting. These people live frugally, yet they would share their last grains of tea or rice with you if you were to pay them a visit."

He pulled up at a little wooden gate leading up to a small unpainted wooden house. Against it huddled a greenhouse. Both buildings appeared to be clinging to the side of the hill for dear life. The notice on a post at the side of the gate said Maniki Flower Garden.

"I won't be a minute."

Kirk left the car to stride along the garden path where he was met by a small middle-aged man in muddy boots and faded cotton trousers and jacket. He bowed low and Kirk spoke to him. Almost at once a small doll-like creature appeared beside him. Papa-san and daughter-san, thought Laurel, thinking how lovely and dainty were the Japanese girls almost without exception.

This little creature smiled up at Kirk like a bright little blackbird, comprehending his request intelligently before scuttling away between rows of staked dahlias and gladioli.

Kirk stood hands in pockets, a carelessly at ease figure, talking to the little market gardener. He was no doubt bowled over by Kirk's charm, Laurel mused, watching the sun glint on the thick crop of crisp dark hair and the wide shoulders. Just looking at him brought a surge of longing for his arms about her and his grey eyes alight with something more than his tolerant teasing.

Presently daughter-san appeared with a bouquet beautifully arranged and tied with ribbon. Money changed hands amid much bowing and smiling and Kirk was returning with the bouquet.

Laurel's colour deepened as he gave it to her with a mocking smile.

"For me? How nice! Thank you, Kirk. They're lovely."

The dew still clung to the delicate petals of the sweet peas, larkspur dahlias and chrysanthemums as she buried her face in them.

"We have a lot of courting to make up," he said, smiling at her pleasure. "Letters are unsatisfactory things."

Better than nothing, though, Laurel thought, and so very, very precious to keep for all time. Her whole being seemed to reach out to him with the premonitory pain that loving, unloved, brings. His thoughtfulness touched her to the verge of tears.

Before lunch Kirk parked the car and they strolled to see the great famous Buddha of Infinite Light over seven feet high and weighing over a hundred tons. It squatted in the open with legs in yoga style and hands palms upwards, thumbs touching in its lap. It had sat there for hundreds of years since the fourteenth century like a great rock untouched by eruptions and progress of time.

Kirk grinned down at her. "How would you like that in your back garden?"

Laurel quipped in return, "There wouldn't be much light about it if we had it near the house!"

There was much to see in the ancient town of Kamakura, but Kirk, after driving along an avenue of pine, bright azalea shrubs and cherry trees for Laurel to gaze up at a shrine reached by seventy steps, told her that other historic places of interest would be left for another day.

They had lunch at a Japanese inn enchanting in structure and design. Kirk ordered a knife and fork for Laurel, knowing she would find it difficult with the chopsticks. She did try and they laughed at her efforts.·

"Not bad for the first time," he said with a chuckle. "I'll teach you."

There was a tender undertone in his teasing which probed her defences. But although he sounded sincere, his smile did not always reach his eyes. His attitude puzzled her until she wanted to ask him point blank why he had married her. The violence of her own feelings astonished her.

She said quietly, "I'm always willing to learn," in such a cool little voice that she wondered if she was really getting as adept as he was at hiding her true feelings.

The afternoon was spent on their own little strip of beach below the garden. They bathed in the warm sunlit water, then stretched out blissfully in the sun. Closing her eyes, Laurel was reminded of the time they had first met when Kirk had taken her with her mother to the coast. They had been much closer then than they were now.

Kirk lay close beside her – too close. If she were to turn her head she would see his dark hair all tousled and drying in the sun, the fringe of his lashes dark against the gleaming bronze of his face and his firm lips closed. The silence around them was profound and restful, yet Laurel felt anything but. Maybe her inner restlessness transmitted itself to him, for she felt him move and bend over her.

"Laurel," he breathed. Not "darling" or any other term of endearment, just "Laurel." Yet the way he said it was like a deep note of music playing on her heart strings. She held her breath with a sense of painful delight deepening the longing inside her which his nearness was making unbearable.

Then his dark head shut out the light and the feel of his mouth on her own stifled everything but the mad beating of her heart beneath his own. The kiss deepened and became urgent, demanding. He let her go at last, very slowly. Neither of them spoke. Laurel felt in her despair that he could not love her or he would not have been satisfied with one kiss.

I love him so much, she thought. I always will. But even as she admitted it there was a conviction that she was reaching out for something that could never be hers. For delicious moments she had imagined her love creating an answering passion in him. Now she knew she had nothing to give that he wanted.

"I'm anxious about you, my sweet," he whispered, hovering over her. "You know that, don't you?"

"I think I understand," she said flatly.

He shook his head. "You don't. Not entirely because you're not a man. You have to trust me and go along with what I do."

He was right – she did not understand him. All she knew was that she loved him and yearned for him with all her being. He had not kissed her lightly or carelessly, Laurel was sure of that. So what was this conflict in him, this awful barrier keeping them apart? Laurel looked up into his face. Poignantly, for breathless moments, their gaze held, lingering with emptiness. The air grew chilly and she shuddered. Instantly, Kirk was looking at the black clouds scuttling along overhead.

"I felt rain," he said shortly. "We'd better go."

Helping her to her feet, he helped her to button up the long skirt and pretty top of her beach suit over her swim-suit. Then.

carelessly shrugging into his bathrobe, he scooped up all the paraphernalia and taking her elbow piloted her towards the house.

Tears blinded her and she stumbled as they reached the little wicket gate leading into the garden. His grip on her elbow steadied her and he frowned down into her pale face.

"Bad head?"

Laurel managed a pale smile. "It will pass."

They went through the little gate. She had not lied, for the tension she had been under had made her temples throb. At the door of the house, Kirk knelt down to change first her shoes, then his own. Leaving the things he was carrying right there, he scooped her up into his arms and carried her into her room. Depositing her on the bed, he unbuttoned the top and long skirt and put her into bed in her brief swim-suit.

"Did Uncle George give you any tablets for these occasions?" he asked as he tucked her into bed.

"They're in a bottle on the bedside table – antibiotics. I don't take them if I can help it."

He strode to the bathroom and was back in seconds with a tumbler of water. Reaching for the capsules, he took one and, sitting sideways beside her on the bed, put an arm around her to lift her up. Obediently, Laurel took the capsule with a drink of water, wishing it had the power to put her out for ever as he held her to him. It was a relief when he lowered her down and left her.

Then he was back again, this time to place something deliciously cold on her burning forehead – a cold compress.

"That better?"

She nodded.

"Go to sleep. You have all of three hours before dinner this evening. Ring for Yuseku if you want anything. I shall be in my room in any case catching up with my correspondence."

He bent to kiss her hair and left the room. The pattering of the rain on the roof must have lulled her to sleep, because the next thing she knew was that Kirk was there looking down at her thoughtfully.

"Had a good sleep?" he asked, taking her slender wrist between thumb and finger.

The sight of his tanned face and keen grey eyes brought a glow of comfort to her trembling heart. But she hoped he would not put down her galloping pulse to his presence. She smiled up at him from clear blue eyes from which all pain had gone and he straightened to stare down at her for a long moment.

"Feel fit enough to get up for dinner?"

"I feel fine."

He hesitated for a moment. "Want any help to dress or wash?"

"No, thanks. I can manage."

He was amused at her sudden vehemence. Laurel made no attempt to get up. For some reason she was shy of leaving her bed in his presence, which was ridiculous seeing that she had spent the afternoon in his presence in her swim-suit.

"Take your time getting up. You have an hour in which to get ready. It's now seven. Dinner is at eight."

He left her then. He had spoken with an easy tolerance. The kiss on the beach had meant nothing to him, she thought. He had been in the kind of mood to seek distraction and had given way briefly to deeper feelings. He might even have imagined she was Nina. Laurel drew a deep breath. She had never felt so oppressed, so hopeless. The fact that he did not love her remained like a stone in her heart.

CHAPTER FIVE

KIRK was waiting for her in the dining room. He turned from
contemplating the view at the window and Laurel was seized
by a new and unaccountable feeling of dread. Was it the subtle
suggestion of strength and obstinacy in his dark sardonic face?
In repose it looked anything but reassuring to her wavering
heart. He had the look of a man who was strong enough to be
patient in order to get what he wanted, the kind who never
gave up. Was that how he felt about Countess Nina?

Her eyes lingered on his mouth and a faint colour stained
her cheeks as she remembered his kiss. His eyes looked straight
into hers and there was something pitiless, something almost
brutal in their regard. Then he moved with that ease and grace
that was characteristic of him and came forward smiling.

"All right?" he asked.

She nodded, aware of his look of appraisal as he seated her
at the dining table. There were chopsticks with the usual cut-
lery. The meal began with a delicious ice-cold soup followed
by chicken with rice and fresh vegetables. The next course
were small slices of raw fish covered by a thick sauce.

"This is where you try the chopsticks," Kirk said with a
quick quirk of amusement at Laurel's stare at her plate. "They're
easy enough to use when you've once got the idea. But first
something to help you to enjoy your Japanese food – saké, the
Japanese national drink made from rice." He filled two tiny
cups with the transparent liquid and passed her one. "This is
the real saké, matured in a cask of cedar wood which gives

it its delightful flavour." He held his cup aloft. "Cheers."

Laurel followed suit. "*Kampai*," she murmured.

He lifted an attractive brow. "So we speak in Japanese. Do you know what that means?"

"It means 'your health' as a toast."

"Clever girl!"

Laurel was surprised at the warm glow after she had drunk the saké. It was quite pleasant.

"Like it?"

She nodded. "Very nice."

He had tossed his down. "Taken in small amounts like this it adds to the enjoyment of the food. It hasn't the kick of spirits, but it is not unlike sherry in its potency." He refilled her cup and came round to stand behind her chair. Leaning over her with an arm each side, he placed her chopsticks in her hands and closing his fingers over hers manipulated them. A portion of the food was conveyed to her mouth and she discovered that the fresh fish was extremely palatable with the sauce. Eventually, her portion disappeared from her plate, washed down by the tiny cups of saké. During the performance her sense of humour had got the better of her and the ripple of mirth bursting from her lips joined Kirk's deep chuckle.

Back in his chair, he grinned at her. "How was it?"

"Not bad at all. Thanks for the lesson."

There was a flicker of approval in his grey eyes. "You're an apt pupil."

"You're a good teacher."

"Thanks. That's comforting."

Laurel caught her breath a little and foced herself to meet his gaze.

"That sounds as though I had a lot to learn."

"So you have," laconically.

"You mean about Japan?"

65

"Japan and other things."

He did not enlarge on what the other things might be. Instead he talked about things in general, disarming her completely. She recalled his words when they sat in the lounge later listening to a radiogram. Kirk had put on a long-playing record of Grieg's music and they sat opposite to each other because he had lighted a cigarette.

At least, Laurel thought that was his reason for not sitting beside her on the settee, to keep the smoke away from her. A kind of rumble came first as the floor shook and the chair trembled beneath her. She looked up at the chandelier swinging perilously from side to side, the dolls did a kind of minuet in the lacquer cabinet and the clock on the mantelpiece did a kind of victory roll before halfway along the shift.

Laurel gripped the arms of her chair, tremblingly aware that something terrible was happening. She was experiencing the sort of shock of one, who, on seeing a mouse, leaps on the nearest chandelier, only this one was swinging madly to and fro like the pendulum of a clock.

The room did a rock and roll quite out of time to the music and Laurel sent an agonizing look at Kirk. He was sitting smoking. His whole attitude was one of complete relaxation, only there was something about him, an indefinable something which calmed her fears and kept her rigid in her chair.

A sudden severe tilt of the room was the last straw. It sent the arm of the record player hurtling across the record, distorting the sound into a wild shriek which somehow mingled with Laurel's. The silence which followed was profound. Kirk had scooped her up into his arms and was now sitting in her chair with her on his knee. She was clinging to him with her face buried in his chest and he was holding her close.

For a long time Laurel knew she was the only one who was trembling. The room had ceased to do so. Everything was static once more.

"Poor sweet," Kirk whispered in her hair. "Your first earthquake."

"Is that what it was?"

Her voice was muffled against him, but she still clung and trembled. His arms tightened around her and they stayed like that for some time, silent and close.

Then he said quietly, "I'm not going to say I'm sorry for not telling you about them. The best way to find about the earthquakes is to experience them at first hand. Had I warned you what to expect you would have imagined all kinds of horror, whereas they're just part of everyday life in Japan. If I'm sorry at all it's for bringing you out here before you were fit to deal with this kind of thing." He gave a short laugh which held no mirth. "You sat there looking at me like a terrified child." Laurel felt his kiss on her hair. "Feel better now?"

"Yes, thanks."

Laurel had stopped trembling, although being held closely in his arms was hardly conducive to utter calm.

"It was only a baby earthquake." His voice was reassuring. "If you look around the room you'll see that nothing has been broken and that things are only out of place. Remarkable when you come to think about it."

Laurel lifted her head and looked around the room. Nothing had been broken. No plaster had fallen from the ceiling, everything was intact. The portrait of Nina had slipped perilously to the edge of the baby grand piano. Her presence in the room seemed almost tangible.

She looked away, made an effort to be normal. "You did right not to tell me about the earthquakes. I would certainly have been on edge waiting for my first one. I'm glad you were with me, though."

He drew her against him. "There'll be many more, but you'll get used to them. There's less risk of wooden houses built on piles of collapsing than those built of brick and cement with cellar foundations. The biggest hazard is fires. Again these people have a wonderful system of battling with them." His lips moved down to her cheek. "Not sorry you came, are you?"

His mouth was seeking hers. He kissed the corner of it. The next moment he would have kissed her. But Laurel could not bear a kiss given to comfort her distress. She turned her face away. He had probably felt her stiffen, although his hold on her remained perfectly still. Confusion swept over her in waves of despair. Her mouth was dry as she sought an excuse for her action.

"I can hear the radiogram still running. Hadn't you better see to it?"

Kirk looked down at her, his face strangely set. "Oh yes," he said with an ominous quietness. "We mustn't forget the radiogram. It's most important."

Wincing at the sarcasm in his voice, Laurel felt herself released. She stood up and he strode across the room, looking up darkly from his task when Yuseku tapped on the door.

Curtly, Kirk bade him enter. With his round yellow face beaming, Yuseku-san gave the kind of glance around the room which sums everything up in a couple of seconds and began to restore order. In his swift noiseless way he went around the room putting it to rights in a manner born of experience.

"Coffee?" he asked brightly, when he had finished.

"Please. Make it good and strong," Kirk commanded.

Yuseku went on a bow and Laurel said swiftly, "Not for me, thanks. I think I'll go to bed."

Kirk closed the lid of the radiogram and straightened. "Sure you won't have a drink of coffee laced with brandy? It would do you good, settle your nerves and make you sleep."

Laurel shook her head. "No, thanks. Goodnight."

He strode across to the door and opened it for her. "Goodnight. Sleep well. There won't be any more eruptions tonight."

CHAPTER SIX

AFTER the earthquake Laurel was prepared for anything. According to Kirk, spring in Japan usually brought a spell of fine weather. It did that week of their honeymoon, making it possible for them to go out on all kind of jaunts. They dined out most nights at Western and Japanese eating places.

Laurel learned to use her chopsticks and she really enjoyed most of the Japanese dishes. She enjoyed the *sukiyaki* dinner taken in the company of other diners sitting on tatami matting minus shoes around a low table. Watching the meal being prepared was an entertainment in itself, with the lady presiding over it looking very charming in her colourful kimono and bright silk obi around her tiny waist.

First, in a heated iron pan over a charcoal brazier, a soy sauce was made into which was cooked a potpourri of meats, vegetables and herbs. Eaten with chopsticks and washed down with saké, it was very palatable. Laurel, flushed with saké and using her chopsticks to good account, would meet Kirk's mocking grey gaze and feel that life was good.

The parks, to Laurel, were enchanting places at their best in the spring with the cherry blossom in full bloom. More enchanting still were the endless crowds of schoolchildren who were always about with their teachers sightseeing and learning all about their country. They would crowd around anyone like Laurel and Kirk to practise their English, the girls in their little pleated skirts and sailor collars, the boys in black suits and small caps on black hair.

They laughed easily with their small almond-shaped eyes disappearing into slits in the round little faces. They cluttered up the park among the many stalls and sideshows, buying candy floss, local sweets and marine delicacies from nearby seaside resorts, and added to the atmosphere of lightheartedness and gaiety.

Laurel blossomed in the sun like a spring flower, her clear eyes glowed and her skin had a pearly transparency of health. Most of the time was spent outdoors swimming, sailing and sightseeing away from the city beneath vast blue skies. She was caught in an enchanting wave of happiness that without wish or volition of her own swept her into a sea of bliss.

Kirk was the ideal companion, lazily tolerant, unperturbed yet giving the impression of smouldering fires underneath. He looked at her often, broodingly, intently, as though he was studying a mathematical problem. Yet his manner was infectiously gay, a surface gaiety not without an endearing devilment.

The nights ended on the same routine of him striding to the adjoining room with a finality which struck a chill to her heart. So the honeymoon ended. Kirk stowed their luggage in the boot of the car and Laurel, from the open car window, breathed in for the last time the air from the garden tinged with the tang of the sea, wet moss and pine, a mingled scent, bitter sweet.

Their new house was in the suburbs of the city which they reached in record time after an uneventful drive. The suburbs were lovely with avenues of stately cedars, cherry trees and acacias. Suddenly it seemed to Laurel's enchanted eyes that the avenues became a garden brilliant with flowering shrubs, superb trees and blossom-laden branches thick as snow.

Looking eagerly through the car window, she saw the roof of the house curling up gaily at the edges as though smiling a welcome. Long carpets of grass set along an elegant avenue of trees led them between the double gates along a drive. Kirk drew up smoothly at the front door. The house, set against a background of wooded hills, overlooked a delightful valley. Down below the lake lay like a discarded mirror reflecting the blue sky and trees etched black on the surface.

If Laurel thought the house they had just left exquisite, she was spellbound by her new home and its setting. It was a semicircular building facing the sun and cuddling the willow pattern garden which appeared to stray over the patios into the house. And what a garden, treated as a gift from the gods and planned with Japanese artistry. Water tinkled merrily over lovingly laid stones, little bamboo bridges and fringed trees studied their reflection in the water surrounded by flowers, rocks and green velvet lawns, a quintessence of subtle perfume and poignant beauty.

Laurel held her breath with delight and shone up at Kirk, who stood beside her watching her enchanting small face.

"I'm speechless. Oh, Kirk, it's heavenly!"

"I thought you'd like it." He laughed easily and lightly. His grey eyes teased. "You can make what alterations you wish, of course. Japanese tradition demands that a house is built with sloping ground in front and the hills behind. The front must face a south-westerly direction, as this is looked upon as the gateway between heaven and earth. In Japanese it's called *jinmom*, meaning man's gateway to heaven."

He followed Laurel's gaze to the letters carved over the door: *Sakura*.

Laurel's soft mouth quivered. Absurd that his voice even when he said words he might or might not mean should do things to her heart to cause her such intense pain. It was not how he looked that counted. It was what he was. He had a rare quality of abundant energy, a magnetism that changed the atmosphere. His charm was immense, heightening all impressions, vitalizing feelings. No matter what he said or did, she loved him, would always love him.

She stared up at his dark intent face. Then he framed her face in his hands and his lips came down on her in a hard kiss. Her mouth responded sweetly to his demanding lips. He felt her tremble as the magic got through to her. When he released her, Laurel was aware without seeing it of his battered quizzical smile.

"I've waited a long time for this moment, Mrs. Kirk Graham. Welcome home!"

Again she had nothing to say. Her lips felt bruised, as bruised as her heart. Yet when he picked her up in his arms to carry her over the threshold with the mocking comment that the occasion still called for it since this was their real home, Laurel had to fight the urge to put her arms around his neck and kiss that mocking mouth.

If beauty was outside the house it was surely within, a cool elegant beauty of highly polished wooden floors covered by oriental rugs in delicate pastel colours. Flowers were everywhere, in floor vases, in exquisite bowls, tall graceful gladioli, feathery fern, magnolias, enchanting twigs arranged with a master hand. Their subtle perfume and delicate artistry appealed to Laurel's sensitive perception, becoming part of her innermost being. Suddenly a door to their left in the hall slid along and a houseboy entered. A classical study in black and white, he came forward noiselessly in heelless slippers. His intelligent yellow face creased into a smile which revealed several gold teeth among a perfect set. He bowed low from the waist, presenting a shiny cap of black hair trimmed neatly in his neck above the white immaculate jacket.

Kirk said, "Laurel, this is Reko who was with me in my bachelor quarters. Reko, my wife, Laurel."

73

Laurel smiled warmly and inclined her head to acknowledge his bow. The Japanese, it seemed, did not shake hands. She had seen the look amounting to hero-worship Reko had given Kirk, who towered above them both, lean-hipped, broad of shoulder with eyes as grey as an English winter.

While Reko went to carry in their luggage, Kirk escorted Laurel on a tour of the house. The kitchen, behind the door through which Reko had entered, was light, airy and scrupulously clean.

Kirk said, "Like most Japanese homes we have electricity for lighting. Cooking is done with charcoal and we have a refrigerator." Leading off from the kitchen was the pantry and food stores. The dining room came next, overlooking the garden, then the lounge and next to that Kirk's study.

Here, there were the usual booklined walls, desk and comfortable chairs. On the desk was a pile of correspondence and Kirk strode to this to sort it out quickly and efficiently. As he did so a small envelope fluttered to the ground at Laurel's feet. She bent to pick up the perfumed letter with a sense of foreboding. A woman's handwriting without a doubt, and a Japanese postmark. Countess Nina's! Laurel could only hazard a guess as she passed it to him with trembling fingers.

"Thanks, my sweet," he said, pushing it absentmindedly in to his inside pocket with the air of a man whose thoughts were elsewhere. To Laurel, the careless acceptance of the letter and the way he had segregated it from the rest was condemnation enough.

Her face had paled. She drew back. The action, rather than the letter, was hurting her more than she would have dreamed possible. He put down his mail.

"You all right, my sweet? You've gone very pale."

He gripped her small cold hands and, although Laurel recoiled inwardly from his touch, something radiantly proud came into her small face. In a small voice, cool and smooth as silk, she said, "I'm all right."

If Laurel had envisaged his past at all it was to imagine him striding through a sequence of trivial love affairs, a few pretty girls, the usual college dances and the fun of blind dates. He was a man now with a man's feeling and passion. So far, Laurel had not seen the passion. But it was there, nevertheless, somehow linked with the perfumed letter lying near his heart.

"You're tired. Come along, let's have tea. Reko will have made it by now. We can see the rest of the house later. There's no hurry."

He put an arm around her shoulders and they went to the lounge. Reko was there within minutes with the lacquer tray. Kirk placed a low table in front of the settee as easily as he had placed Laurel on it. Reko put down the tray and Kirk took over.

Unhappily, Laurel tried not to think of the letter in his pocket and accepted her tea. The lounge window, like all the others, looked out over the garden. It opened on a patio and everything looked beautifully peaceful, but Laurel was discovering that the heart could know torture even in beautiful surroundings.

The tea was refreshing. They had lunched on the way back to Tokyo, so neither of them was inclined to eat the little delicacies Reko had brought in along with the tea. Kirk had a cigarette.

He was studying the glowing tip when he said casually, "I don't expect you to settle in here right away. You're sure to feel a bit restless. I know how you're feeling." His tender smile down at her was loaded with charm. "It must have been an appalling ordeal losing your parents in such tragic circumstances. The aftermath was pretty rough too. The kind of illness you had always leaves a certain amount of depression. Fortunately, we have a good doctor on hand, a personal friend of mine. He and his wife were away in Germany when we got married, so they were unable to attend. Otherwise you would have met him."

Laurel put down her empty cup. "I don't need a doctor, Kirk. I'm well. It's . . . as you say, a matter of adjusting myself to a new life." She shook her head as he picked up the teapot to replenish her cup. "No more, thanks."

He stubbed out his cigarette into an ashtray on the lacquer table, said carefully as if he had already said too much, "We have a Japanese room – I know you'll want to see that right away. Shall we go?"

Laurel was on her feet eager to be moving. Somehow being alone with Kirk only increased her restlessness. He had risen too to look down at her with an expression which she could not read, searching, quizzical. There seemed to be a trace of bitter humour and she wondered why.

Like the other rooms, the Japanese room overlooked the garded through a wall consisting of sliding floor-to-ceiling glass doors. A cool, bar room of pale walls where nothing was contrived but where everything was plain to see. The yellowish green, thick tatami mats with their surface of very finely woven rushes stretched over a base of crude rice straw harmonised with the mellowed tones of the room. On the inner wall facing the garden was an alcove with a step containing an arrangement of twigs rather like pussy willow in an elegant vase. Above it all on the wall was a painting of Mount Fujiyama.

"Every Japanese has a similar alcove," explained Kirk. "It's called a *tokonoma*. Years ago it was used for sleeping in, being warmer than sleeping on the floor of the room. The floors were then concrete. Now they're wooden and much warmer. The built-in cupboards around the walls contain cushions for sitting on, also the brazier, kettle and things for the tea ceremony."

Laurel shone up at him, thoroughly interested. "I'm aching

76

to see you in a kimono. I suppose that's why the men wear them, because they're easier to sit down in."

"They are warmer too in the winter worn in layers. I have a kimono. I wore it for judo and karate, for which I hold the black belt. Personally I prefer my own clothes, but you'll look delicious in a kimono with your dainty figure and tiny waist. Most Western women buy one. They can't resist the beauty of them."

He left her at the door of the first bedroom. "There are four bedrooms. This one is yours and mine. I'll leave you now to unpack. Dinner is at eight, but I shall see you before then."

Laurel entered the prettiest room she had ever seen, magnolia walls with touches of palest pink, in the dainty lace bedcover, in the pillows and sheets, in the beautiful wall clock and in the pretty arrangement of tea-roses in a vase on her bedside table. There was a card propped up against the gold and cream bedside lamp.

"To my darling wife. All my love, Kirk."

How could he? Laurel crushed the card in her hand. With misty eyes she looked around the room to stare at the pink and white silk corded bell rope beside the bed. Everything laid on, she thought bitterly, even to a tasselled bell rope to summon morning tea. Then she stared down at the card in her hand. She was too weak-willed to destroy it, of course. Despising herself, she straightened it out and put it into the dressing table drawer.

It was a few minutes before she began to unpack. It occurred to her long before she had finished that Kirk's suitcases were not there. Here we go again, she thought, in the other room. Leaving the empty cases to be taken away by Reko, Laurel left the room to peep into the next bedroom. This one was more austere, with a bedroom suite in dark wood contrasting dramatically against pale walls. The cream wool bedspread was unadorned and the masculine set of hairbrushes, her wedding present to Kirk, mocked her from the dressing table.

Laurel had not the heart to look in at the other two bedrooms. Returning to her room, she washed off the dust of travel in a bath of warm water perfumed from the cut glass bottles and jars arrayed beautifully along glass shelves. Here again she felt the subtle touch of a woman. Who, Countess Nina? Laurel pondered, dressing mechanically. Kirk had not said whether there would be guests for dinner so, to be on the safe side, she chose an elegant slim-fitting black velvet dress with extravagantly simple high-fitting bodice painstakingly made from tiers of white lace. She dressed her shining coils of hair Grecian-style on her head, adding make-up lightly, a whisper of blue to her eyes, lipstick and a dusting of powder. The ruffle of blue lace around her slim throat did away with the need for a necklace, but the small cameo, her mother's looked demure at her throat.

Kirk would, no doubt, be wearing a lounge suit if they were dining alone. But the dress gave Laurel confidence; besides, it would be good practice for when they did entertain or go out to dine with his friends. No doubt he had been regarded as being one of the most eligible Englishmen in Tokyo and she had carried him off right under the pretty noses of all the women who would have been angling for him. Her cheeks warmed at the thought of meeting their critical gaze.

The effect upon Kirk as she entered the dining room was balm to her sore heart. A swift gleam in the grey eyes, enough to electrify the atmosphere, was gone before she could swear it had been there at all.

"You look lovely, my sweet."

He caught her hands as he strode forward. She felt his arms around her and they kissed. He released her quickly.

She hesitated, began, "I didn't know if we were to have guests or not." Her blue eyes, bewildered and unhappy, took in his grey lounge suit. "You didn't. . . ."

"I'm sorry, I ought to have told you. Don't look so upset." His sardonic grin relegated her concern to the depths. "Is it so surprising to want you to myself on our first evening home?"

He took her hand to lead her to a low table containing two parcels.

"We've received a great many wedding presents which we shall have to go through some time in the future. These two are from the Emperor. I thought we'd better see what they are before putting them away. All the presents have been acknowledged. These arrived while we were away."

Both parcels were wrapped in the manner of Japanese wedding gifts tied with the traditional knot in white and gold cord and a paper *noshi*, the Japanese sign of a gift. There was also the royal insignia. Kirk parted the wrappings on the first to reveal two beautiful cloisonné vases.

"Very nice," was his bland comment.

"They're lovely," murmured Laurel wistfully.

The enclosed card was rather a splendid affair in gold headed with the Imperial crown. From their Imperial Majesties the Emperor and Empress.

The smaller parcel contained a bottle of saké and three diminutive cups. Kirk replaced the lid of this rather quickly and minus a smile, but not before he had read the extra words written by hand on the card enclosed.

"What did the card say?" Laurel asked curiously, thinking it odd he had not let her see it

He shrugged. "A little joke between the Emperor and myself. I'll tell you about it some time."

Laurel flinched inwardly. She felt as though a door had been

79

slammed in her face. She took it on the chin. "How nice of their majesties. We shall have to thank them."

"They've already been thanked. The Emperor is away." He pinched her cheek. "He'll receive his wedding cake when he returns."

She gave a small laugh. It was either that or cry. "Just like that," flippantly. So far she had only taken part in the wedding ceremony. Had it not occurred to him that it was her wedding as well as his and that she would have found pleasure in acknowledging the gifts herself? Apparently it had not. The eyes she raised to his were bright with unshed tears. "Remind me to have you at my next wedding."

She turned away then to blink back the tears and was totally unprepared for the savage grip on her shoulders as he swung her round to face him.

He spoke with impersonal and hard deliberateness. "Don't ever say that again, even in jest. What I have I hold."

He kissed her then. It was the kind of kiss Laurel could not define, like no other she had ever received. There was no love or desire in it, only plain cold anger. It told her she was his as long as it suited his purpose. It seemed to go on and on, bruising her lips as well as her heart. A discreet tap on the door parted them, and Reko entered to say that dinner was ready.

The dinner was perfect. Reko, with a snow-white napkin on one arm, trod silently about the table offering the superbly cooked food, the beer, ice chilled for Kirk, the sherry for Laurel. Later they went into the lounge for coffee and Kirk, into her lap as she sat down on the settee.

"Our photograph album of the wedding," he said dryly. "It arrived today."

Laurel took it from him with a gasp of pleasure as she admired the gold tassel down the spine and the gilt-edged pages. "Ours?"

Her look was so unbelieving, he laughed. "Who else?"

He lowered his long length beside her and Laurel bit her lip. The New Otami Hotel took care of everything where weddings were concerned, she knew. But they would not prepare a wedding album of the photographs unless specially requested to do so. Kirk had obviously requested it and his thoughtfulness touched her and made her feel too full for words. Her hands trembled as she opened it. They looked at it together, Kirk with an arm along the back of the settee behind her, his face close to her hair as he looked down.

All the photographs were excellent and the two tiny bridesmaids looked delicious. The one showing them cutting the cake caught at her heart. Kirk, with that smile of extraordinary charm, was the devoted bridegroom, gazing down at her absorption of the task in hand with a look of tenderness which Laurel felt was assured solely to impress.

"There are several pictures of the wedding in the Japanese magazines. One in particular has exclusive pictures of the house and garden and an article on the furnishings. I've ordered them for you."

Kirk told her this later as they strolled in the garden before going to bed. The moonlight splashed inky shadows beneath the trees, the perfume of the garden was the essence of things Oriental, stinging the nostrils and stirring the emotions to a vague yet drowsy excitement. The sky was sapphire, casting a blue haze over the lake, and the hills gave a sense of unreality in the hazy background. To Laurel it was a dream world, an ideal place for two lovers who had been parted to meet and find their dreams come true.

Nature could not have presented a richer, more wonderful bit of heaven than this garden of Eden in which they walked.

But behind all the perfection of the time, the place and the loved one together was the shadow of a wall as impenetrable as a light through thick fog. It drew closer and closer around her, affecting her both mentally and physically, attaining substance.

Kirk had spoken seldom and was completely unobtrusive as if he was aware of her secret longing for him and was avoiding any action that might fan it into flame. He was smoking a cigarette and was gazing out across the valley. A breath of tobacco wafted towards her and she watched his arrogant profile, held by a creeping fascination. The situation was incredible. It could not go on, she told herself wildly.

Presently he crushed out the cigarette with his heel and smiled down at her. "One of the most wonderful things about you is that you don't talk a man to death. It's so restful to be with you." His grey eyes raked her face. "You're beginning to look much better since you arrived."

"Am I?" tonelessly. She clenched her hands.

"Don't you feel better?"

The shadow was still there between his own gravely searching eyes and her wretched ones. Suddenly she could not bear it.

"I ... I ..." Laurel stopped, unable to go on, and to her horror she began to weep hopelessly and quietly as she had done in the weeks following her mother's death, her face in her hands.

"Stop it," Doctor Machelle had commanded her sternly when he had found her in tears. "This kind of thing is no good for your recovery."

Now Kirk was saying it. "Stop it, Laurel!" He said it firmly and harshly yet with a gentleness beneath the harshness. He drew her against him. "This isn't like you. You've always been such a brave little thing, sticking to your determination to nurse your mother against all odds. You'll get over it." He kissed her hair. "Don't want to go back to England, do you?

You're not homesick?"

She shook her head against him. Gradually she grew quiet.

"Laurel." He spoke her name gently like a caress. "This is something we have to face together. You can face it if I can. You can trust me to do the right thing. We do belong to each other, you know.'

Laurel used her handkerchief. "I'm sorry," she said in a husky voice. "I think I'll go to bed."

"Yes. I'll come along with you." He put an arm around her shoulders and they walked back to the house.

Reko met them in the garden – Kirk was wanted on the phone. Instantly he was on the alert.

"Thanks, Reko. I was expecting it. I'll take it in my study." His smile down at Laurel was apologetic. "Shan't be long, my sweet."

The next moment he had gone, with his graceful long stride.

Laurel stayed where he had left her; the emotion with which she was filled was unbearable. All kinds of thoughts were seething through her brain, thoughts of Kirk and Nina – unfair thoughts? She had to find out. If it was not Nina, he would have taken the call in the hall. But no, it had to be in his study where no one could hear.

Mechanically, her footsteps were guided in that direction, working along to where the study window overlooked the garden. He was there inside at the phone. Laurel drew back against the side of the window in the shadows.

He was saying, "What you suggest, Nina, is impossible. I know you're eager to get it over, but you must leave it to me. I have to see it through myself. We must think of Ishi and there must be no scandal." A pause. "I agree. It does put me in an intolerable position, but there's nothing I can do about it. You must see that." Another pause. "No," very firmly. "That's the last thing you must do. You'll have to be patient. I'll be back at the office on Monday. We can discuss it then. . . ."

Laurel did not wait to hear any more. She had heard enough. She paused at the door before entering the house to pull herself together. He attitude was one of utter dejection. It was clear enough even to her way of thinking that Kirk had married her for a purpose. But what purpose?

Things were, perhaps, more painful because she was so physically near him, sleeping in the next room; it intensified the fact that he made no effort to break down the wall of reserve between them. In fact, he might be, where personal contact was concerned, a hundred miles away.

Thinking about this, Laurel, who had been standing with closed eyes in melancholy contemplation of her intolerable position, opened them to see Kirk standing on the threshold of the door.

"Sorry about that," he said. "Come to the lounge for a nightcap to make you sleep."

Pale, unsmiling, like a stone statue, Laurel felt him take her cold hand and lead her through into the hall.

"I'd rather go to bed. I'm tired," she said, and even her voice sounded like a stranger's.

Kirk had spoken in level teasing tones. Now he was frowning down at her, puzzled at the coldness of her look. "Are you?" He smiled. "Well, don't be too serious about it. You know I won't disturb you. I know you have to get well before we begin our married life together in earnest."

Laurel looked up at his dark face. The conversation she had just heard had ploughed a painful furrow through her brain until it hurt unbearably. Exasperation mingled with her pain and the torment of loving him blocked her throat.

"Get well?" she echoed blankly, two perpendicular lines appearing between her delicate brows.

He gestured with a hand as though she was behaving stupidly. "Didn't Uncle George say anything to you about taking things easy for a while?"

"He gave me tranquillizers, if that's what you mean."

Kirk gazed down for a long moment into her unhappy eyes and a wave of compassion made him speak very gently as though to a child. "Forget it. Go to bed. Goodnight – sleep well."

Laurel never remembered how she got to her room. Awareness came back when she lay in bed, smothering her tearless sobs of anguish into the pillow.

CHAPTER SEVEN

IT was eight o'clock when Laurel opened her eyes. She lay hovering between sleep and wakefulness, listening to the chatter of the birds outside her window and the soft brushing of dew wet leaves against the panes.

Myopically, she gazed around the beautiful dreamy room, looking tender and undisturbed with the pretty window curtains framing the beginning of a new day. Sunshine sent beams of dancing gold dust across her bed and voices from the garden cleared her brain of the last remnants of sleep. Reaching for her negligée, a frothy lace and ribbon affair to match her nightgown, Laurel slipped it on and went to the window.

Reko was there talking to a man in faded cotton trousers and jacket. He was digging, bending over his spade to show the black hair curled up into a duck's tail in his neck. He was tubby and elderly and was obviously the new gardener. Reko went indoors and the man bent down to take up a piece of the newly dug soil and break it gently, almost reverently in his fingers.

Laurel watched him with a tender smile. Really large farms did not exist in Japan. Most of them, she knew, were no more than an acre and small enough to work by hand. The poor gardener probably did not possess even an acre. He could belong to one of the families to be seen tending the narrow tracts of land no more than six feet wide which rose in shallow tiers on the slopes.

She walked to the bathroom thoughtfully, taking in the luxury of shell pink and black ornate fittings, fluffy rich towels and the gleam of tiled walls. What a hard life the Japanese peasants enjoyed compared with this! Yet they smiled so readily even when up to their knees in ice-cold muddy water in their rice paddies. Could it be that in the very simplicity and humbleness of their existence they had found the key to real happiness?

Even with her own problems still unsolved, Laurel was beginning to feel the utter tranquillity, the sense of infinite quiet and unity creeping into her being like a healing balm. She cleaned her teeth, ignoring the fact that the bathroom looked too feminine in the morning light without Kirk's shavng tackle and toothbrush.

She had not heard him leave in the car to go to his first day back at his office. No doubt he had, though after peeping into her room to find her still sleeping. Laurel dressed thinking of the duties she would have to undertake as his wife, entertaining his friends and colleagues and visiting them in their homes. She was not looking forward to it, although she had reconciled herself to living one day at a time until her problems resolved themselves.

She was ready when a tap came on her door and Kirk entered in a smartly cut dark city-going suit and pale blue shirt which did something to his grey eyes and bronze skin.

"Good morning, my sweet. Ready for breakfast?" He bent his dark head and kissed her lips lightly. "Hmm, you smell delicious."

He exuded a freshly groomed masculine fragrance. Was it cedar soap? And was he as pleased to see her as he looked?

"So you do," she said, adding hurriedly at the pained expression her remark put on his face, "In a masculine way, of course."

"Thanks," his grey eyes laughed down at her. "Did you sleep well?"

"So-so. Aren't you going to your office this morning?"

"Yes, after I've had breakfast with my wife."

"But won't it make you late?"

"Undoubtedly. However, since it will be the first time I shall manage to arrive before they recover from the shock. We're having breakfast on the patio. It's warm enough and you'll enjoy it."

The early morning meal with Kirk in a teasing mood and a panoramic view of Tokyo at her feet was heaven to Laurel. The city was surrounded by thick walls and numerous shallow moats stapled with bridges. To Laurel, it was one of the most beautiful places she had ever seen, with its wooded hills and valleys, quaint buildings and small doll-like dwellings set amidst pines, weeping willows and cherry blossom. She gazed at it entranced until, aware of Kirk's eyes on her, she turned to meet his intent look.

His charm was irresistible when he chose. "Come on, you can do better than that. You're eating nothing. The view is hardly as sustaining as breakfast, so eat, there's a good girl."

He pushed a dish of fruit towards her and refilled her cup. He ate what he wanted and lighted a cigarette. Laurel looked at the strong brown throat as he sent a line of smoke heavenwards.

"You'll be used to the views by now. To me they're new and enchanting. I don't imagine myself ever looking at them and remaining unmoved by their beauty," she said.

She peeled a banana and he smiled at her lazily. "I agree. I love this country and all the fundamental values simmering beneath the surface which only people who live here can really feel. I've never felt an alien and, while I keep very much to myself, I feel part of the community. By the way, the building reaching for the sky on yonder hill behind the trees is the Imperial Palace of the Emperor."

He indicated the roofs of a magnificent building perched regally in isolated splendour on the top of green slopes surrounded by shallow moats. It was half hidden by a boskage of trees and high walls. Grassy banks sloped from the walls down to the moat. They were planted with willow and cherry blossom, some of which gave the impression of having slipped down to the edge of the water to bend Narcissus-fashion to admire their own reflections. Swans cruised elegantly along on the water beneath them and the high walls surrounding the palace had wide gateways at intervals with carved wooden gates and brass fittings.

Laurel said, "Isn't the Emperor supposed to be a divine being to his subjects?"

"Not so much since the last war," he answered lazily. "Before then he was looked upon as something out of this world and practically indestructible. The war changed all that by proving he was as prone to destruction as his subjects. You'll enjoy making his acquaintance."

"You mean we shall go to the Imperial Palace?"

"The Emperor is away, but the Empress is at home. You'll probably be requested to go to tea."

In her mind's eye Laurel saw Countess Nina looking at her patronizingly with the mocking regard of a woman who had nothing to fear from Kirk's wife. The woman's affair with Kirk would be court gossip, and Laurel shrank from the thought of meeting all the critical eyes.

"Do I have to go?" she almost pleaded.

"Naturally. What are you afraid of? Your taste in dress is impeccable, you have that quiet and enviable quality of speech and manner of which the Japanese so highly approve. You're also slim, dainty and pretty." He tapped ash from his cigarette into an ashtray on the low table and leaned back again in his chair to survey her with approval. "Pretty enough to hold your own against the best of them. You'll have a store of beautiful memories in years to come because I can assure you that you'll enjoy yourself here.

"Things are changing here fast, but we in the Diplomatic Service have the privilege of moving in the old Japan which the Imperial Palace still holds almost intact." He smiled with a gleam in his eyes which made Laurel's heart turn in her breast. "By the way, Japanese women are by age-long tradition obedient and subservient to their husbands."

"But how dull for the husband to have a wife who's afraid to say bo to a goose!"

"Do you think so?"

"Of course I do. How can one respect a doormat? Half the fun of marriage is the battle of wills between husband and wife."

"Really?" lifting a quizzical brow. "Sounds interesting. Tell me more."

Laurel saw his lips twitch and was sunk. He has got me absolutely, ran the devious tenor of her thoughts. It's something bigger than myself ... like the air I breathe ... my life's blood, my whole being.

"Why should I make it harder for myself by letting you know my opinions on the subject?"

"Touché," he said lightly. "Do I detect a challenge? Can it be possible that my sweet fragile-looking wife is both passionate and chaste?" He threw back his head and laughed at the sudden rush of colour staining her cheeks to a wild rose. "It's not fair to tease you. The important thing at the moment is to see you don't get bored being on your own while I'm at the office. I'm buying you a horse. I remember you saying you used to help a neighbour sometimes with her riding stable.

My horse is stabled with friends at the moment until we have a stable built here."

Laurel felt the prick of tears behind her eyes. How much more did he remember? Did he ever think of those all too brief ecstatic hours they had spent together a year ago, how happy they had been. Now his feelings were more or less under lock and key. She had once possessed that key and could not, even now, believe she had lost it.

"I'd like that," she said evenly. "I did a bit of riding when I went down to Cornwall after my illness."

"Good. Riding will be more relaxing for you than driving a car at the moment. Fortunately, we have the summer to look forward to and you can go swimming in the lake and take a book to laze in the sun. I shall feel easier knowing you're near home for the first week or so. Reko will be here and a woman is coming in every day to do a few chores, so you won't be alone." He smiled, a tender smile transforming his dark sardonic face in which the grey eyes allured and startled and made her heart beat in thick deep strokes. "As for the earth tremors, they will persist, I'm afraid, owing to the alluvial soil. Think you can stand them?"

She nodded. "I think so. I've never been afraid of thunder and lightning, so I suppose I'll get used to them. Anyway, I love the country."

"That will help, because you can regard the rumblings as being some kind of message from the earth saying it reciprocates your love."

Achingly, Laurel wanted him to add, as I do. Why don't you tell me that you love me? her heart cried piteously. Then I can face earthquakes and anything else, however terrifying. In the ensuing agonizing moments she ceased to draw breath, so great was her longing. But she could not reach him. A sob rose from deep down inside her as he looked at his wrist watch,

91

then stubbed out his cigarette.

"Duty calls. Feeling all right now?"

He was on his feet, pushing back his chair and towering above her. In spite of his height and breadth of shoulder, his hard leanness and experienced charm, he looked so boyishly endearing, so unconsciously aware of her love for him that Laurel loved him more in that moment than she had ever done.

"Yes, thanks."

His mouth gave a cynical twist and he shoved his hands into his pockets.

"The Japanese have a saying which means bend with the wind. I think it helps."

Laurel felt a lump in her throat as big as a goose egg. "Thanks, I'll remember that." Her smile was wavering.

He grimaced wryly and continued to contemplate her, his eyes narrowing.

"I'd like to see you smile more," he said gravely. "Don't come to see me off. I'll have to rush. Relax and look at the papers. See you at lunch."

He planted a kiss on the top of her head and was gone.

Among the morning papers Laurel found a glossy magazine. To her surprise, the picture on the cover was that of their new home. Inside were further pictures and an article about their marriage. She was deeply interested in it when Reko came in to announce their first visitor.

The Countess Wanaka. Hastily, Laurel smoothed her hair and made her way to the lounge. A young woman in a beautiful kimono in pale grey embroidered in white flowers with a pale pink obi around her slim waist bowed as she entered. For several seconds the two women eyed each other with no change of expression.

Laurel found herself looking at the original of the photograph that had watched her groping through her honeymoon, constituting an ever-present threat to her own happiness. Laurel's first astounding thought was that Countess Nina was not really beautiful. She was the kind who was photogenic. She gave an instant impression of beauty because she knew how to use every trick to its best advantage. Her skin had the oriental texture of a ripe peach. Her slanting eyes, amber and dark-lashed, her rather retroussê nose and full lips added up to a strange face, a sensuous face that riveted and demanded attention.

"Countess Wanaka?" Laurel smiled pleasantly as* the woman bowed. "I feel I already know you from the photograph on the piano at your home. It was kind of you to lend us the house. Please sit down."

"Not at all. Kirk is a very close friend of ours." Nina sat down gracefully in a chair while Laurel took one opposite. "Ishi adores him."

A strange feeling of crisis made Laurel choose her words carefully.

"I believe you've been to the hot springs at Norebetsu? I hope your husband feels a benefit from his visit there?"

Between the thick black lashes came a calculated gleam of amber. Small white teeth showed in a smile that was no smile Perceptively, Nina's voice hardened. The American accent became more marked.

"Ishi is quite well. The Japanese males look after themselves well – or rather they see that their wives do."

"You're American?"

"I was. Since knowing your husband I realize what I've missed in marrying a Japanese." Nina gave her a long speculative look from under curling lashes. "You don't know how lucky you are, Mrs. Graham."

"Thank you." Laurel maintained a steady look.

93

Beneath it, Nina said amiably, "Actually, I came to see Kirk."

"Surely you knew he would be at his office this morning?"

"Of course. That's why I'm here."

Laurel smiled. "I don't understand."

"Its quite simple," Nina vouchsafed as if Laurel was a complete idiot. "My husband is a Minister for the Interior and we have a town house not far from the government building in Tokyo. It was important for me to see Kirk this morning and I rang up his office to find he had not arrived. I rang the house to find the line engaged, so I decided then to come to see him."

"But why all the haste?"

"Kirk has never been late for work before. It was most unusual."

Nina had taken off her gloves to show magnificent rings on her fingers which flashed in the sun filling the room.

Laurel watched their glitter. "I'm sorry you missed Kirk. I'm also surprised that you didn't wait for him at his office. Reko would be using the phone when you rang here to order provisions, most likely."

"I'm afraid I'm a little impulsive and I didn't pause to think," Nina said smoothly. "You see, Kirk has always been such a close friend of mine and I was hoping his marriage would not interfere with our friendship."

Laurel kept her eyes now on the other woman's calm mask of a face. She disliked her and her kind, her beautiful insolence, her brazenness in trailing after another woman's husband when she was married herself.

Her smile was sweet, almost gracious. "You must see that having a single man for a friend is not the same as having a married one. Naturally, his wife will come first. I see no reason, though, why you shouldn't remain friends providing

94

your friendship is kept within bounds. Actually, it was my fault that Kirk was late at his office this morning."

Nina's smirk was one of satisfaction. "I knew it was no fault of Kirk's. He's much too exacting in his work to show any signs of weakness."

"Being late for work is hardly a sign of weakness in a married man. Often unforeseen circumstances arise – the wife could be indisposed or there could be a baby on the way."

The amber eyes narrowed, the peach bloom face darkened in colour. "I would hardly think the latter was so in your case, Mrs. Graham, though I've heard that you are very much the invalid. I trust it won't injure Kirk's career. He's very highly thought of in diplomatic circles and he has a great future."

Laurel's heart plunged painfully. "Indeed?" She felt bewildered, but her quick wit was busily assessing the strength of the grapevine encircling the English community. Like every other country it thrived on gossip.

Nina made a gesture with a perfectly manicured hand, flashing her rings to give weight to her words.

"Surely that was why Kirk guarded you like a hothouse plant before you were married? He was so careful to keep you away from prying eyes or anything in the least upsetting."

Laurel met her amber eyes calmly. "There could have been other reasons. He could have wanted me to himself. After all, we were apart for a long time."

"Exactly."

Cold air rippled over her skin. "What do you mean?"

"For a man who wanted to keep you to himself, he behaved very oddly."

Pale with anger and disgust, Laurel said quietly, "In what way?"

"Kirk had two months' leave coming to him, yet he only

95

took one week of it for his honeymoon. Doesn't that strike you as odd?"

"There could be a reason."

The woman's words had filled the air of the quiet room with a venom from which Laurel recoiled. For a moment she was angry, then common sense prevailed. A sense of humour was called for in a situation like this. Her visitor had been trying to make her angry, to loosen her tongue and thus let out the true relationship between her and Kirk. So far Nina could only guess at it.

Nina smiled, well pleased with the way the conversation was going.

"I hope we can be friends. I have an influential position at court – in fact our house comes under the protection of the Imperial Palace. I can do much for you."

"So it seems," Laurel said dryly. "Thanks for the offer, but I'm sure I shall get along admirably as Kirk's wife. As you mentioned earlier, a man who is destined for a great career can surely take care of his own wife. I must apologize for not offering you refreshment, but it's a little early and you're in a hurry to see Kirk, so I won't detain you. Good day, Countess Wanaka. Reko will see you out."

Laurel walked to the door, opened it and gave a short gracious bow. She was trembling when the woman rose to her feet with a look of hauteur and swept to the door, passing her with an icy cold travesty of a smile.

Laurel had gone to her room when Reko knocked with a glass of milk and rice biscuits. Kirk had apparently left his orders. She sat down by her window to drink, but left the biscuits. Nina would now be going post-haste to Kirk's office. Maybe she ought to have treated the woman with an amused tolerance, but it was not in Laurel's make-up to pretend friendship where none existed. Her own courage, her respect for others demanded the same respect for herself. This woman had none.

If Nina was having an affair with Kirk, and it certainly looked that way, then she would fight it at any cost. Whether her love for Kirk would be the same afterwards was something to be proved. Refusing to be browbeaten by such a woman, Laurel thought despairingly how a man could be so blind as to a woman's true colours. They probably found it out too late.

Kirk did not come home to lunch. He rang up to say he could not make it. After lunch, Laurel wrote several letters home, including one to Kirk's uncle George, Doctor Machelle. In it she told him how wonderful the country was, thanked him for the cheque he had sent for their wedding present and altogether wrote like a happy bride.

Three o'clock brought two more visitors, the two voices she had overheard on the morning of her wedding in the hairdressing salon. And although they were responsible for much of her heartache and the disruption of her marriage, Laurel liked them on sight. To begin with they looked so comical together when she entered the lounge that she was inclined to giggle.

One was tall and rangy with brown hair and horn-rimmed spectacles covering grey eyes set in a long sallow face. Her companion was small, plump and blonde, rather like a robin in her suit of cherry red. For a fleeting moment Laurel imagined them in kimonos. The result was so hilarious that she found herself suppressing a chuckle.

"Good afternoon," said the tall one. "We hope you don't mind us calling. Kirk rang me up and asked us to call. He thought you might feel lonely on your first day at home. We met at the wedding, but you'd be too bemused to remember us." She smiled, her brown eyes warm with friendliness. "I'm

Jean Summers and this is Susan Smithers."

Laurel shook hands with them. "How nice of you to call. Please sit down and I'll ring for tea."

But Reko was there as if on cue, setting down the tray between Laurel and her guests on a low table. Laurel dispensed tea and cakes. Jean had a cigarette and Susan, like Laurel, was content to nibble at the small delicious cakes.

Jean's husband Dennis managed one of the big international banks in Tokyo. Susan's husband, a writer, was working on the memoirs of a well-known Japanese man of letters.

"Think you'll like it here?" Jean asked amiably, leaning back in her chair and exhaling smoke carefully away from her companions.

"It's a beautiful, strange country, but one in which I'm beginning to feel at home," Laurel vouchsafed.

"My husband Bill and I love it here," Susan said, finishing her fourth little cake with an air of satisfaction. "There's heaps to do – golfing, tennis, sailing, climbing, riding, badminton, even hops in a helicopter."

Jean agreed. "There are lots of laughs on the way too if you look for them. The laughter wrinkles I've encouraged since coming here don't bear thinking about – as if my marriage lines aren't enough!" Her smile emphasized the wrinkles on her good-natured face. "I'm thirty-five, Susan is twenty-four, more about your age, Laurel. May I call you Laurel?"

"By all means."

If Countess Nina had sent her spirits down to zero Jean and Susan had sent them up again with mercurial swiftness. On Christian name terms, they got on like a house on fire.

Jean started her third cigarette. "We're all going on a climb of Mount Fujiyama this weekend. Has Kirk told you about it?"

Laurel shook her head. "No. It sounds fun. I suppose Kirk is an expert at it."

"Kirk is an expert at anything," Jean vouchsafed without rancour. "He's good fun to be with too, never gets in a panic in emergency and is completely unperturbed by caustic remarks, adverse weather conditions or any other obstacle which would make another man hesitate. You're going to be regarded with envy by all the females around, including several in kimonos."

Laurel smiled. "Do you think I'll survive?"

"Kirk married you, didn't he?" Susan took a breath between chewing her fifth cake. "I'm glad he married you. We're going to be great friends."

Jean was amused at Laurel's sudden flush. "Susan's right. You have nothing to worry about regarding Kirk being a good husband. He's the kind we all dreamed of marrying – goodlooking, tolerant, humorous and a perfect gent. He'll treat you like a precious piece of porcelain. I'm not surprised he's chosen someone like you, sweet and unspoiled. He's seen so many of the other kind – in his own circle, I mean. Frankly, you were lucky to come out here and find him still single. These little Japanese women, for instance, can charm the ducks off the water. They wait upon their husbands hand and foot, are hardworking, artistic and have never heard of Women's Lib."

"They will do," chipped in Susan darkly.

Before her guests left, Laurel escorted them around the house. A surprise came for her when, on taking them to see the bedroom, she discovered that the third was a nursery.

"Very nice," Jean said, her amused glance flickering over the pretty bamboo cot with its frilly drapes tied with blue ribbon. "Blue for a boy too! Trust Kirk to presume the first-born will be. He'll get his wish too, I'll be bound."

Laurel had another peep into the nursery when they had gone, gazing around it wistfully. All part of the set-up, of course. And yet this room did not seem to have Countess Nina's touch. Maybe she had not been consulted about the furnishings after all.

Steady on, Laurel admonished herself, your visitors have sent you up in the clouds. Nothing has changed you and Kirk. But he did ask them to come and see me, she argued. And they saw nothing odd in having a week's honeymoon. After the unpleasant incident with Nina that morning, her feelings had verged on despair. Now, in a new light mood, Laurel felt years older in experience and not so shattered.

The light mood persisted when she dressed for dinner that evening in the black silk flowered trouser suit. She was ready when the slam of Kirk's car door heralded his arrival. Quivering a little despite her determination to remain calm, Laurel waited for his footsteps. Would they pass her door or would he peep in to see her?

She heard him greeting Reko, the short conversation, then his footsteps passing her door. Some of the spirit went out of her then. Leaving her room, she went to the lounge to fetch the glossy magazine containing photographs and an account of their new home. It would be something to keep in later years of a marriage that never was, Laurel told herself bitterly.

Back in her room, she waited for Kirk to leave his and opened her door.

"Hello there," he said breezily. "Sorry I couldn't make it for lunch. Had a nice day?"

His arm was around her slim shoulders and they strolled to the dining room. To Laurel's sensitive perception there was a strange undercurrent as though Kirk was being charmingly polite against his will.

"Yes, thanks," coolly. "It was kind of you to ask Jean and Susan to call."

"I thought you would enjoy their company." He led her

into the dining room and seated her at the table.

"I did, very much."

Laurel spoke with lowered lids, shaking out her table napkin, aware of his well tended flexible fingers doing likewise in the seat opposite.

"They're both intelligent and sensible young women. You'll find them good friends. Their husbands are equally likeable." Kirk raised his eyes across the table to meet her blue ones. "They have bikes as well as cars, so I suppose you'll be wanting the same."

Laurel met his mocking gaze and wished he did not look so critical. Was that the word? Funny she should feel something about her displeased him. He had not mentioned his reason for not coming home to lunch; but she knew instinctively that he had dined with Nina.

"A bicycle sounds fun, and they're popular here," she said evenly.

Reko came in with the first course and went out again. Kirk picked up his soup spoon. "There's plenty of time. Some of the roads are deplorable, especially in rainy weather. You can take things easy for a while. I expect you will be making changes about the house. I want you to go ahead in that respect and do whatever you want. The shopping facilities in Tokyo are wide and varied. What you can't get we can always send away for."

Laurel's lips, stiff and cold, curved to receive her soup. In some strange way the house and its contents did not seem to have anything to do with her. Everything went on oiled wheels without her help. Reko was up at five every morning, going through the household chores like a clean breeze before preparing breakfast. The soiled laundry was taken away and returned beautifully done in a matter of hours. Her own underwear, put out that morning, now lay in softly perfumed folds

101

in her bedroom drawers.

How was she ever going to get close to Kirk without sharing any intimate little pleasures like trying out a new recipe and waiting to see his reaction? She looked down at the golden-brown portion of chicken Reko was placing beside her plate. It was perfectly cooked. So were the vegetables she added to her plate.

"I shall have to look around before I dare to make any alterations. In fact, there's so much beauty both indoors and out that I feel I can never improve upon it," she said, passing him the vegetable dish.

Kirk leaned over to add more vegetables to her portion. "'That's better. See you eat it." Taking his own share, he put down the dish and continued with the conversation. "Even so, a house no matter how excellently furnished invariably needs the woman's touch."

They ate in silence. Laurel was thinking of Nina and wondering why he had not mentioned her visit that morning. He must know she had been to the house. Yet for the life of her she could not mention it, nor her surprise on seeing the nursery. They were in the lounge having coffee when Kirk mentioned the Countess.

His first words, clipped and to the point, jolted her severely. "Why were you so rude to Countess Wanaka this morning?"

Laurel's nerves stretched to shrieking point. Although she had expected him to mention the visit, the accusation came like a bolt from the blue.

"I beg your pardon?" she said with youthful dignity.

"I asked you why you were so rude to a friend of mine this morning," he repeated with the air of a man being reasonable against his will.

She put down her coffee cup with trembling hands. "Since you're convinced that I'm the guilty party, why not ask her?"

"I don't remember saying you were to blame," he said with a dangerous quietness.

"No, but your manner implies it. Your precious Nina. . . ."

He cut in sharply, "She's not my precious Nina!"

"No?" Laurel was deathly pale and shaking. The only colour in her face was her eyes dark with indignation and anguish. "Strange I should have that impression, just as you have that I'm to blame."

Kirk was studying the glowing tip of his cigarette. He was a little pinched about the nostrils, a sure sign that he was angry. But he controlled himself, leaning forward to flick ash from his cigarette into the ash tray on the low table.

"Maybe I deserve that," he admitted evenly, leaning back in his chair to look at her angry eyes. "While the last thing I want is to upset you I must know what went on. I didn't mention it before because I wanted you to enjoy your dinner. You can't afford to miss a meal because you don't eat enough as it is. Nina was most upset when she came to my office this morning. Apparently you were hostile from the moment she arrived."

"Then that made two of us. To begin with, she didn't come to see me, she came to see you."

"Laurel! How can you say that a woman who couldn't wait to welcome you and make friends?" He spoke sternly.

She rose to her feet, hands clenched by her sides. She looked young and vulnerable, but there was a quiet dignity about her forlorn slim figure that was infinitely touching.

"The woman came here to meet you and to make mischief — I can see that now. And you had lunch with her after she'd maligned me instead of coming home."

His face darkened at the contempt in her clear voice. "I can't see what that has to do with it."

Laurel laughed — it was either that or cry. "You only see

103

what you want to see." She drew herself up to her full height and took a deep breath. "Well, let me tell you this, Kirk Graham, had it been the other way round and a man friend of mine had made accusations against you, the last thing I would have done would have been to dine with him afterwards. So drink that down with your coffee."

Her voice wavered on the last word and she ran from the room. She heard him call her name as she ran, and once in the haven of her room she locked her door, leaning back against it and trembling uncontrollably. Sweat oozed on her temples like dew and the palms of her hands were damp with moisture.

How could he take that woman's part against her? The silence mocked as she threw herself on the bed to stare up at the ceiling. Kirk had not followed her. If only he had, to show that he cared about her! Taken her into his arms and given her the love she so badly needed from him.

Laurel closed her eyes, too cut to the heart to cry.

"Laurel, I want to talk to you."

Kirk's voice, accompanied by a rap on the door, came through the mists of sleep. She opened her eyes to a darkened room and memory stabbed like knives.

Another peremptory tap at the door and Kirk's voice demanding entry made her push herself up into a sitting position on the bed. Wearily, Laurel put a hand up to her head.

"Go away! You've already made up your mind who you want to believe. Now leave me alone," she said.

Another turn of the door knob, then silence. Laurel lay down again and wept.

CHAPTER EIGHT

Nothing ever seems so bad in the morning light, thought Laurel, awakening to find that it was eight o'clock. She had overslept, which meant that Kirk would have left the house for his office. Hastily, she left her bed to unlock the door, hoping Reko had not been with her early morning tea to find it locked. Whatever happened no breath of scandal must be circulated about her marriage. Not that Reko was likely to talk. He was much too devoted to Kirk to hurt him in any way. He came with her breakfast as though he had been listening for the sound of the unlocking of her door. There was a note on the tray from Kirk.

It read, "Have a good lie in this morning and take things easy. I shall be home to lunch. Kirk."

But Laurel was not the staying in bed type. In any case, she felt much too restless to stay immobile. The first round of a battle with Nina had not been very successful. Nothing had been solved. Going for a walk to think things over, Laurel strolled along leafy lanes looking out on panoramic views.

Little smoke signals spiralled up into the blue sky from bonfires of dead winter grass, along the banks of a stream. Here and there fishermen balanced precariously on rocks tried their luck in the shallow waters. On the slopes the narrow paddy fields were beautifully sown and tended and down in the valley small figures moved across a golf course, their bright red and yellow golf bags giving a gay touch of colour to the scene.

Laurel saw it all vaguely as in a dream. Her thoughts were confused. It was so difficult to know what to do for the best. If she had been rude to Nina it had been the woman's own fault as much as her own. I could have been more diplomatic about it, she mused. Yet her more chastened mood did nothing to bolster her morale at the thought of meeting Kirk at lunch time.

The walk up the mountain pass in the laughing sunshine took on new dimensions. Gradually, Laurel relaxed to gaze on the most surprising views as peak after peak of the hills rose before her. Then they were forgotten in the breathtaking view of distant Fujiyama, white, dazzling, an unforgettable cone-shaped image piercing the blue sky. Thick mists swirled around the base rising again to cover its modesty. Entranced, Laurel wondered if she had really seen it and she continued with wings on her feet along the narrow mountain road.

The little brown house appeared as if by magic around a bend in the road. The room was open to the garden and inside a girl in a pretty kimono was toasting bread on chopsticks over a charcoal fire. Laurel watched fascinated by the delicate movements of her hands. Now she was making the tea and suddenly looking up and across the small garden to where Laurel stood.

Ashamed of herself for being so rude as to stare, she turned away after a little apologetic smile and hurriedly retraced her steps homeward. The touch of a hand on her arm halted her and the girl with black shiny built up hair and a merry face was gesturing for her to walk back again into the house.

Laurel was by now feeling a little exhausted and the offer of tea proved too much. Willingly, she allowed the girl to take her back. She shed her shoes at the door and walked on the soft tatami mats to sit on a bright silk cushion. The tray, in the form of a lotus leaf, held the teapot and matching cups painted gaily with birds flying over mountain peaks.

While she plied Laurel with tea and the delicious crisp brown toast, she talked about herself. Her name was O-mea, she was sixteen and looked after an old lady who was bedridden in the house. She seldom saw anyone except the tradesmen and it was heaven to see Laurel. She did sketches in her spare time and she fetched her sketchbook for Laurel to see.

It was not until they had sat down that Laurel discovered O-mea could speak English. Shyness had kept her silent until then. The sketches were good and the girl obviously had talent. Time went on wings, till Laurel realized with dismay that she would have to hurry to get back home in time for lunch.

"*Sayonara*," cried O-mea, waving her on her way and standing in the road until Laurel turned a corner out of sight. Fortunately, the road back was downhill. She had run until she saw the roofs of the house and something more. Kirk was walking nonchalantly up the mountain pass to meet her. The incline, however, was too steep for her to slow down and she found herself hurtling down into his arms.

For blissful moments her slim suppleness was pressed against him as she took in deep breaths to replenish her lungs. He felt the fragrance of her hair beneath his lips before she lifted her head.

"Oh!" she exclaimed on a breathy laugh. "I'm so sorry I ran into you like that. Am I late for lunch?"

He looked down at the warm smooth rose of her cheeks, her bright eyes, her soft throat and the pink mouth slightly open to help her breathing. Then he was bending his head and quietly, gently was kissing her. For a moment she stood tense, and trembled.

He let her go, his face revealing nothing of his feelings. But his slow lazy smile rocked her heart.

"No, you're not late," he said, placing an arm around her shoulder as they walked on. "I came to look for you, only too pleased that you're out enjoying the fresh air. You look blooming."

The rose flush deepened. "Do I?"

To cover her embarrassment, Laurel told him about seeing Mount Fujiyama and taking tea with O-mea, then, not wishing to bore him, she spoke about the golf links they were now looking down on in the valley below. As a bachelor he would go freely to play as the mood took him. Was he already chaffing against the bonds of matrimony which were anything but satisfactory in their present state?

"That looks a very good golf course down there. Are you a keen golfer?" she asked tentatively.

He tossed a negligent glance in that direction. "Not particularly. It's only one of my many pursuits. As you enjoy most of my activities we shall in future share them."

"Are we going climbing this weekend?"

His glance was quizzical. "You know about it?"

"Yes. Jean and Susan mentioned it when they were here."

"Done any climbing?"

"No, but it sounds fun."

"You will enjoy it. Although it can prove exhausting on a hot day. Fortunately, we have the cool spring weather as yet. I've been up myself on more than one occasion when I felt the need for solitude."

The incidence of the previous day was forgotten as he talked about climbing. To Laurel's relief he did not allude to it during lunch, a lunch which he took control of, slicing cold meat and putting a generous portion on her plate. There was a poignant sweetness at being taken care of by Kirk.

"I've a surprise for you," he told her. "You're summoned to the Imperial Palace tomorrow afternoon to meet the Empress."

Laurel watched him dumbly as she reached across to pile salad on her plate. The tea and toast mid-morning had already taken the edge off her appetite. Now this.

"Oh dear!" she cried.

He put down the salad bowl after taking some himself and Laurel knew her eyes betrayed her utter dismay.

"It's quite an informal gathering," he vouchsafed, adding a delicious sauce to his plate. "You really ought to try this sauce."

She shook her head. "I shall go with you, of course."

"I'm afraid not." He smiled at her reassuringly. "It's an afternoon tea party for a few pretty ladies, yourself included." A pause. "Countess Nina is to present you to Her Highness."

"I see." The temperature in the room took a decided plunge. "What shall I wear? It's rather short notice, isn't it?"

He grinned. "Not in Japan. They can produce a tailored suit in under twenty-four hours. Which reminds me," Kirk slipped a hand inside his jacket pocket and drew out a cheque book made out in her name, "there you are. You can buy anything you wish." He pushed it across the table.

She stared at it woodenly. "Thanks."

"Don't look so worried," he teased. "I'm going to take you to a sweet little lady who'll make you a suitable dress. She's a court dressmaker and knows exactly what is required. I'll drive you there after lunch on my way back to the office. We can call at the Imperial Palace on the way to give you a closer look at it!"

On the green waters of the moat surrounding the Imperial Palace, the swans looked beautifully white as Kirk drove to the Ohte gate. Laurel was aware of pine-clad slopes, massive grey masonry and white watchtowers. The usual daily sightseers were there taking pictures of the grounds through the bars of the closed gates.

Kirk was instantly recognised by the black uniformed guards who saluted and allowed him to drive through the huge gateway to follow a fifteen-foot-thick high stone wall topped by a watchtower. This curved round to a large lawn where cars were already parked. Kirk parked the car and they strolled beneath trees laden by cherry blossom looking like blobs of snow through which the sun frolicked.

The grounds were really lovely. Kirk had said they would have time for a quick look around, so they did not linger until Laurel heard the sound of men's voices and a spate of stentorian laughter. It was coming from a field behind tall pines and there was sudden glimpses of gay colours worn by men on horseback. There were eight of them, four clad in red coats and white shirts and four in blue jackets and pink shirts.

"Polo players," Laurel said. "They have long bamboo poles with nets on the end."

Kirk was grinning down at her. "I know."

"You play polo?"

He nodded. "Another of my vices," he mocked.

She said, "I know so little about you."

"You know enough," was the cool reply. "Come along, we shall have to go."

"Does the Emperor play polo?"

They were back in the car approaching the gates when Laurel asked the question. Kirk did not answer. He was leaning out of the car window having a word with the uniformed guards at the gates. He spoke swiftly in Japanese and they replied, showing gold teeth among white ones as they saluted.

Evidently they had shared a joke, for Kirk grinned as he returned their salute and shot through the massive gateway.

"You were saying?" he said as they left the palace behind and joined the traffic on the main highway.

"It was nothing," she answered, thinking that playing polo could be a cover-up for his affair with Nina. The ladies of the court would be spectators, naturally, and the Countess was sure to be one of them.

Kirk swung the car from the main road towards the suburbs. "It's an awful job to trace anyone here. The numbers of houses are like a jigsaw puzzle. The lord knows how the postmen manage to deliver the letters. The best thing to do if you want to find an address is to go to the police." He slowed down at a crossroads and turned by a tall red post topped by a red light. "This is the road, I think, going by the fire alarm."

Laurel eyed the post apprehensively. "Is that what the red posts are?"

"Yes. We have one in the garden. I'll show you how to use it. They can't afford to play around with fires. The alarm is rung at the slightest suspicion of an outbreak. Like the earthquakes, it's another item of everyday life. Either of these hazards can wipe out a city in no time."

The road wound between yew hedges hiding small picturesque dwellings of unpainted wood. Kirk drew up at the first one. A small garden was surrounded by a fence and a little wicket gate. Leaving the car, Kirk opened the gate to the tinkle of a bell, stood aside for Laurel to enter and escorted her along the garden path.

The garden had the sad dejected look of having battled through a hard winter. Tufts of dead winter grass loomed up between azaleas and the shoots of spring flowers. In a corner by the house a willow tree was sprouting little green shoots along its branches. The bell must have alerted someone in the house, for the sliding door moved and a little Japanese lady stood there.

Mrs. Pakara was a diminutive four foot ten or so. She had the appearance of a well-preserved geisha girl in her forties. She wore a beautiful kimono with a richly embroidered obi around her tiny waist. Her abundant hair and shoe-button eyes were black in a Malay kind of face and her little hands were covered in rings. She reminded Laurel of a bright little bird,

111

but a knowing one who could sum a person up in seconds and keep what she knew under the elaborate hairdo.

Kirk greeted her charmingly with a slight bow and addressed her in Japanese.

As they talked, Mrs. Pakara's bright black eyes flickered over Laurel's slim form as if she was already taking her measurements. Kirk eventually turned to Laurel.

"Mrs. Pakara is very busy, but she'll be happy to make your dress for tomorrow. Mrs. Pakara, my wife Laurel."

Mrs. Pakara bowed low, Laurel bowed and looked up at Kirk.

He smiled down at her reassuringly. "Mrs. Pakara speaks English, so you'll be able to understand each other. I'll leave you with her and pick you up around five."

As he strode away to his car Mrs. Pakara smiled at Laurel. *"Dazo,"* she said with a bow which Laurel knew meant 'please to enter.' Another sliding door faced her as she stepped into the vestibule. Slipping off her shoes, she stepped into a pair awaiting on the step and followed her hostess across a beautifully polished hall.

Inside, the house looked more spacious than it appeared, probably because of the Japanese way of furnishing. Yet another sliding door was pulled along and at a smile from Mrs. Pakara, Laurel removed her shoes and entered to tread on thick tatami mats.

The room was typically Japanese with the elegant spaciousness of walled cupboards and sea of floor. In the far wall was the usual *tokonama* or raised alcove with its beautiful flower arrangement beneath a pictured scroll of a Japanese landscape. In front of this lay a gurgling baby surrounded by cushions. Mrs. Pakara went across to him, raised him on his fat little legs and spoke a few words in Japanese. The next moment he was bending double with his little black head going down to the dimpled chubby hands on the floor in a bow to Laurel.

He was too fat to get up again and rolled over in the cushions chuckling with mirth.

Laurel was captivated. "Isn't he sweet?" she cried.

Mrs. Pakara smiled. "Baby of daughter-san. Name of Fuseko."

Laurel bent down to take hold of one chubby hand and Fuseko pulled himself up into a sitting position. "What does his name mean?" she asked.

"Fuseko means Little Luxury."

Laurel laughed. "A very precious one too!"

"Sons very precious. Daughters not so precious in Japan."

"Then your daughter has made up for her own sex by having this lovely baby. He's delicious." Her smile was tender. "May I pick him up?" She picked him up and cuddled him, loving his small velvety cheek against her own, then put him down as Mrs. Pakara returned armed with rolls of material and a pattern book.

Sitting among cushions on the tatami mats they chose a pattern and a lovely roll of brocade.

Mrs. Pakara said, "This famous Nishijin brocade only used in best fashion houses. I will make it nice for you. You have pretty dainty figure."

The material was draped on Laurel and pinned in all the vital places. It was then whisked off, cut and tried on again. The tiny expert hands moved lovingly over the material, reminding Laurel of the gardener who caressed the lumps of soil. Mrs. Pakara was smiling and chuckling as if she was getting the greatest pleasure out of making the dress. The rings on her hands shone no less brighter than her eyes.

Now and then she would leave the room and sew. Then back again she would come for another fitting. In between these outbursts of energy several callers arrived and it seemed to Laurel that the front gate was forever tinkling.

Mrs. Pakara, however, was undismayed by these interruptions, taking them all in her stride. Eventually the basic lines of the dress were complete.

"Dress ready for tomorrow," Mrs. Pakara promised after a last satisfactory fitting. "We have tea now."

Fuseko or Little Luxury had fallen asleep. In less time than it takes to look around, everything cluttering up the neatness of the room had been put away, rolls of material, snippings of cloth, pins, scissors, tape measure and pattern book disappeared as if by magic.

Quickly the little brazier set in the well of the floor was lighted, the kettle put on, and plates of little cakes brought in. Green tea was poured into eggshell china bowls from a matching teapot and they nibbled cakes as they talked.

Mrs. Pakara was a widow who had outgrown her illusions. Her husband had died after three years of marriage leaving her with a small daughter aged two. Mr. Pakara had owned a bookshop in Tokyo and his wife, having no love or interest in books, had sold it. Now, twenty years later, she was a successful dressmaker.

"Clothes are my life," said Mrs. Pakara, passing more cakes and tea to Laurel. "A plain woman can turn heads if she knows how to wear clothes."

Laurel agreed and the time went on wings. The sound of Kirk arriving brought an end to a visit Laurel had thoroughly enjoyed.

"How did it go?" Kirk asked when they were on their way home.

"It was delightful." The last few hours spent in Mrs. Pakara's company had made her feel alive and on the edge of laughter. "The baby was delicious."

He gave her a swift glance. "You're fond of children?"

114

Kirk was concentrating on his driving among a horde of cyclists.

"I adore them. You certainly charmed Mrs. Pakara into making the dress. A constant string of customers arrived during the afternoon."

"Are you glad? You'll have a beautifully modelled dress fit to be presented at court."

"You might not be so pleased when you hear what it costs. Mrs. Pakara assures me that the brocade is very expensive and only used in the best fashion houses," she said dryly.

"So what?" Kirk had rid himself of the cyclists and was putting on speed. "You like it, don't you?"

"Yes, very much."

"Then there's nothing more to be said."

She eyed him covertly, saw that he looked immensely strong and dynamic. Those steel grey eyes were fixed right ahead. If only he would look at her as she wanted him to look with a need for her that would turn her bones to jelly! She sighed.

"Tired?"

"Goodness, no!"

"I'm glad."

"Are you. Why?"

"You'll see," laconically.

And she did, staring wide-eyed at the cars parked around their house, in the grounds and on the approach road.

"What . . . what are all the cars doing at the house?" she asked huskily.

"A housewarming party. I thought it was better to give you a surprise instead of you worrying about it beforehand. All right?"

She nodded. "I was wondering when you were getting round to it."

Kirk drove in, passing cars up the drive to the cleared entrance to the garage which Reko had kept open. Then, like two conspirators, they left the garage hand in hand to go round to the back of the house and enter by the kitchen garden door. Inside the door they paused as voices came along the corridor from the bedrooms.

He bent his head and whispered urgently, "Visitors leaving their coats in the spare bedrooms. Quick, in here until they've gone, then we can go and change."

He pulled her into a little cupboard affair at the end of the corridor where Reko kept his overalls. They stood close, so close that Laurel could feel the strength of his hard body against her own. Kirk was all fire and laughter, so endearing. He held her against him carelessly, easily. Yet Laurel could not relax, could not be as carefree. How could she when she did not trust him?

"All clear now, I think."

"Yes." Her voice was quite steady. She even managed a smile.

"Hurry and change. I'll join you when I'm ready."

He came to her room eventually to find her struggling with the zip of her evening dress.

"Here, let me." He was across the room in long strides and Laurel with her back to him trembled at the cool touch of his fingers as he worked on the zip. "There you are." The zip ran smoothly up her back. "No, don't turn round. Look into the mirror."

She obeyed, saw the grey eyes above her own that enchanted while they mocked. He had taken something from his pocket and placed it on her dark hair. It was a small tiara with the glitter of a thousand lights. Then he was clipping the long diamond earrings on to the small lobes of her ears.

"My mother's," he said. "A family heirloom for my bride."

Laurel stared speechless at her own dazzling reflection. Her

116

cheeks were the colour of a wild rose, her eyes dark pools of bewilderment.

"But they look valuable. I've never had anything like it in my life!"

His eyes teased her shocked expression of surprise at the beauty of her own image looking wide-eyed back at her from the mirror. "Have they bolstered your morale?" he said softly against one glittering small ear. "I've yet to see a more beautiful hostess about to welcome her guests. Shall we go?"

He held out his arm and she slipped her hand inside it. They walked into a room filled with a bright laughing, chattering crowd which transformed it into something warm and welcoming.

"Here they are," someone said brightly, and the spate of lighthearted chatter was stilled long enough for the guests to swarm around them.

With Laurel beside him, Kirk separated, coupled and introduced guests with his usual imperturbability and charm. Reko was there with several waiters weaving in and out with trays of drinks and everyone seemed settled to join in and enjoy the housewarming party.

A long table was set at one end of the dining room loaded with food for a buffet meal. There were too many to seat them all. Laurel enjoyed it all immensely. Everyone was so warm and friendly and there was none of the critical looks she had dreaded.

Granted, most of the guests had already attended the wedding reception like Jean's husband Dennis. He was blond and very attractive with blue eyes and even features including a Grecian nose and rather weak mouth. His fair hair clustered in small curls over his head and he had the bold looks of a man aware of his own attractions where women were concerned.

117

Susan's husband Bill towered above his wife like a bean-pole, and was pleasantly ugly with a long thin face and looked shy. Champagne bubbled freely and as the evening advanced, Laurel noticed Dennis taking more than was good for him. Furthermore, he had made no secret of his admiration for her. One look from his bold blue eyes made her feel undressed.

Countess Nina had arrived a little late with her husband. She looked ravishing in white and diamonds and her glance at Laurel's exquisite tiara was a cat's gleam of amber between thick lashes.

Her husband Ishi, a handsome distinguished-looking man, could have passed for a European had it not been for his slant-ing full-lidded eyes. They were talking to Kirk when Laurel sauntered into the garden where Reko was attending to the overflow of guests.

She had astonished herself with the ease in which she was able to relax and be her natural self. Her eyes were warmly eloquent and her voice accompanied occasionally by husky laughter was low, sweet and musical as she talked to a young under-secretary of the Imperial court, an official of the Minis-try of Education and an American from the Embassy.

The garden was gay with lanterns and a low sickle moon was appearing in the darkening sky. Later, Laurel retraced her footsteps back to the house by a side path. She saw Nina with a wrap around her shoulders ... saw Kirk join her, heard their quiet laughter, their voices and watched them pass in the shad-ows in the direction of the little wicket gate leading down the slopes to the lake. Her hands clenched at her sides and she drew a deep breath as though mortally wounded. How could Kirk take that woman on a walk she herself had gone with him and treasured? She told herself bitterly that he would not be so detached with his present companion, would not even wait until they reached the seclusion of the lakeside before he took

118

her into his arms.

Laurel was shattered by the intense feelings of jealousy and despair running riot inside her. Unhappiness engulfed her like a choking cloud, drying her throat and clouding her vision. She stood for several moments pulling herself together.

"So this is where you're hiding, in the garden."

Drink-sodden breath fanned her cheek. Someone loomed unsteadily behind her. A voice lowered to her ear, was slurred. Laurel swung round to look up at Jean's husband, much the worse for drink. He was swaying on his feet. The shock of seeing him so cleared her brain as to give her an ice-cold logic.

She smiled, "I've been talking to my guests, Mr. Summers."

He swayed towards her and she put out a hand to steady him.

"Where ... do you get this Mr. Summers from? I'm Dennis. I'm one of your guests too, and I demand your attention."

He looked down on her broodingly. Her hand flat against his chest appeared to be holding him upright.

"Dennis, then," she said lightly. "I didn't mean to offend."

"Don't you like me?"

Laurel recoiled inwardly as he took her hand and raised it to his lips.

"Of course I do. We're friends." She managed a smile, her eyes purely personal, her face serene. "And don't shout," gently. "Come on, sit down."

They were near the patio outside the lounge. Laurel freed her hand and led him to the bamboo chairs placed by a low table.

He dropped heavily into a chair and made a grab for her. She cleverly evaded him. "I'm not shouting. Come here, you lovely thing."

Laurel adroitly took shelter behind the small table. "Oh, but you are. You're going to have a drink."

To her intense relief Reko was there with a tray, blandly smiling.

"Coffee, Okasama?" His light metallic-sounding voice was reassuring.

Her smile registered her grateful thanks. "Yes, please, Reko. Will you put it down on the table? I'll see to it. Thank you."

"Who said anything about coffee?" Dennis growled in disgust.

With steady hands, Laurel poured out a cup of strong black coffee. Dennis accepted it with an ill grace, watching her pour a weaker cup for herself.

"Cheers," she said. "Drink it up like a good boy and tell me about yourself."

To her relief he obeyed and she poured him out a second cup. Gradually, she drew him out of his brooding mood to talk about himself until his eyes closed and he fell asleep.

She met a worried Jean on her way indoors. "If you're looking for Dennis, he's asleep on the patio. I should leave him for a while."

Jean looked immensely relieved. "He hasn't been making a nuisance of himself, has he?"

"Stop worrying. Dennis is enjoying himself. That's what he came for." Laurel linked Jean's arm. "Let's go indoors. I suppose you've seen the housewarming presents?"

"What a nice person you are, Laurel." Jean kissed her cheek. "I know Dennis has had too much to drink. Drink and women are his favourite hobbies."

"We all have our problems," said Laurel.

When the last trickle of guests had gone, she was aware of Nina holding back until the last. Her husband had left earlier in the evening to go to a previous engagement. Laurel had an idea he had gone to keep some date with a geisha girl. Strange she should have that idea of a man she hardly knew. But a great many wealthy Japanese entertained a geisha girl, sometimes taking a favourite one as a concubine.

Reko had brought Nina's wrap and Kirk was helping her on with it. Laurel thanked her for coming, bade her a cool goodnight and went along to her room.

With mixed feelings she walked to the window to look out into the darkness unseeingly, every nerve in her body taut. When she heard someone enter the room, she made no move but stood rigid, a catch in her breath. Colour had fled from her face leaving her skin pale with the luminosity of a pearl in the gloom.

"Laurel," Kirk said softly.

Had she but known it Laurel had never looked so lovely, so desirable, with her wide eloquent eyes dark pools in the paleness of her face. Her red lips quivered as she turned to face him and the small tiara was a blaze of light in the gloom.

"Laurel," he said again, his eyes looking at her meltingly tender. He placed his hand around the top of her slender arms. "You were wonderful tonight."

Laurel stiffened in his hold. Her voice was husky and well chilled.

"Was I?"

He frowned down at her darkly. "Is anything the matter?"

In that moment she almost hated him. "Has Nina gone?" she asked flatly.

"I'm taking her home."

"Are you asking me or telling me?" bitterly.

"Why should I ask you if I can take a friend home?"

"Why should you?" A rush of anger stained her cheeks and she trembled. "Why come in to tell me? You do as you like in any case."

"Of course I do. I allow you to do the same — or haven't you noticed?"

121

"You'd be surprised what I've noticed." Her sarcasm was as heavy as his own. "Why do you make your friendship with that woman so obvious? I heard her refuse two lifts home from guests. I think . . ."

He was savagely angry, she knew, gripping her arms so painfully that she winced, as he cut in. "I don't want to hear your opinion on a matter which doesn't concern you. It's not important."

"It's of the utmost importance, since it does concern me."

"In what way?"

"As your wife. We are supposed to be married."

"There's no supposing about it. We *are* married." He released her and pushed his hands into his pockets, surveying her with an insolent mockery which made her long to slap his face. "However, I lead such a monastic existence that I can hardly be blamed if the fact escapes me from time to time. Can I?"

Standing there before him, Laurel felt his deep emotion, knew him to be labouring under gusts of anger which he held in leash. His frowning black brows gave his dark sardonic face a grimness that was frightening in its intensity. But Laurel was not afraid of him, for a passionate hope was leaping in her breast at his words.

She put out a hand, then drew it back. "You mean Nina is. . . ."

"Nothing to me," he finished for her.

She shook her head. "Nothing?" she repeated woodenly as if trying to convince herself. She stared at him in disbelief and started to tremble.

"Stop it!" Kirk gripped her shoulders. "I married you, didn't I? You have to trust me, or what's our marriage worth? We belong to each other."

Laurel turned away. "Do we? Do you belong to me?"

Suddenly he swung her round, his anger unleashed. "You

122

doubt it? Then let me convince you."

Seizing her in his arms, he took her soft lips, forcing them to obey his own. But she stood passive in his cruel embrace. Suddenly he released her and she was alone.

For a long time after he had gone Laurel stood staring out into the night. Her mouth still burned and she felt bruised and battered when she finally prepared for bed. A slight cut inside her lip was bleeding, so she made do with a mouth wash instead of cleaning her teeth. The double bed seemed king-sized in her utter loneliness as she tossed and turned.

She thought again of Kirk's brutal kiss and because she loved him, Laurel could feel sorry for him. Poor Kirk, loving one woman and married to another. He wanted her to believe there was nothing between them. How could she when his every action pointed to an association with Nina?

It was a well known fact that the Japanese were not in favour of divorce, which could be the reason Nina had not asked for one. She could be biding her time, knowing it would be easy enough for Kirk to get an annulment.

At least I didn't throw myself into his arms, Laurel thought miserably. How easily I could have given way to my love for him, begging him to love me, to make my marriage secure so that no annulment would be possible. But I wouldn't want him on those terms. I might even have had his child. She trembled at the thought. But I won't take him on those terms either, much as I would like a child.

But where to go from here? A burning question, and one which she eventually abandoned in favour of sleep.

CHAPTER NINE

At six o'clock the paper boy whistling on his bicycle awakened Laurel. Drowsily, she listened, then slept. It was seven when she awoke again. In the cheering light of a new day the tumult of feeling brought about by the events of the previous day had subsided into something she could face if not entirely banish.

No one would have guessed the kind of unsettled night she had gone through when she walked into the dining room for breakfast. At least, not Kirk, who was perusing one of the morning papers. Her heart somersaulted as usual at the sight of him.

His face was a gleaming bronze mask, his hair darkened by his recent swim in the lake. She caught in the morning light his speculative look from clear grey eyes and hung on to her play-it-cool rôle with considerable effort. The next moment she was lowering her eyes from that smile of extraordinary charm as he pulled out her chair.

"Good morning, my sweet. You have a full day ahead, I believe. First a visit to your dressmaker, an appointment at the hairdressers and tea in the afternoon at the Imperial Palace. You look bandbox fresh. How are you feeling?"

Laurel sat down and replied that she was feeling all right. He resumed his seat as Reko appeared, relinquished his morning paper and gave his attention to his breakfast and Laurel.

Outwardly they were a normal married couple sharing their first intimate meal of the day together. Kirk was utterly at ease, or so he appeared to be, and gradually his calm got through to her.

124

He was to drive her to Mrs. Pakara's for her dress and from there she was to get a taxi to the hairdressers at the New Atami Hotel, then a taxi home. At eight-fifteen, Laurel was sitting beside Kirk in the big roomy car watching him drive confidently towards the city.

The Japanese were early risers and already the small brown houses they passed had been swept, cleaned and polished. The little concrete vestibule between the two doors had been scrubbed, the path swept and watered. Papers had been collected from the glass-fronted box attached to the front fence, so had the bottles of milk in the gaily painted wooden fixture inside the front gates.

Cycles, hundreds of them, weaved their way in and out of the traffic and mothers clipclopped along in wooden *getas* with their babies strapped on their backs. It seemed to Laurel that every turn of the car wheels revealed a beauty that enchanted. Even in the city one felt the serenity of the old Japan. It lingered like an aura around the Imperial Palace, even among the Western-style office blocks set in the midst of gardens, and even the constant stream of modern traffic failed to dispel it altogether.

Kirk slowed the car as they passed an office block set in immaculate gardens. He gestured towards it with a lean brown hand.

"This is where I work. I'll take you round some time."

Laurel looked wistfully at the place where he spent most of his day.

"It looks very nice," she said inanely. "Why did you decide to work in Japan?"

"My father's influence, I'm afraid. He loved it here. He came to study economics at Tokyo university and stayed to lecture and write. He said Japan had taught him how to live and enjoy life. He liked the way the smiling little people, instead of growing away from nature, had taken it as part of their lives. They encouraged it to flow through their homes like rivers, purifying the unnatural environment indoors which would eventually poison the human element."

"And your mother? Did she share his enthusiasm?"

"Up to a point. She insisted that I should be educated in England. I won enough degrees to secure a job here, and here I am."

"And your father?"

"He was killed two years ago while playing polo. He fell from his horse and was struck on the temple by the hooves of another horse. My mother, who saw it happen, died of shock. They were very devoted."

"I'm so sorry."

"I've got over it now. Looking back on it I realize Mother wouldn't have wanted to go on without my father."

They had reached Mrs. Pakara's house and he dropped her off. Mrs. Pakara was at the door as the gate bell tinkled. She looked stricken. She greeted Laurel politely, looking very attractive this morning in slate grey with a blue glittering obi around her tiny waist.

"*Dazo*," she said. "I sad today."

"You mean my dress isn't finished?" Laurel was slipping off her shoes before entering the hall.

"Yes, dress finished last night. Hope you like."

"Like?" Laurel echoed ten minutes later as she surveyed herself in the beautiful brocade dress. She was standing in front of the full-length mirror in Mrs. Pakara's workroom. It was a perfect fit, emphasising the youthful curves of her slender figure. The silken threads of the material seemed to have woven all the delicate colours of a Japanese landscape in the sheen of it. The obi around her small waist held all the rich colours of a sunset.

"It's beautiful!" Laurel turned to look at a perfect back view. "I've never seen anything so beautiful."

Mrs. Pakara lifted black hopeful eyes still shadowed. "You really like?"

"I adore it. What a dear you are to work so hard in order to get it ready for me. I'll take it off while you make out the bill for me."

Mrs. Pakara had the bill ready and she handed it to Laurel as if she expected her to be shocked by it. The bill was so modest that Laurel gasped.

"Mrs. Pakara, are you sure this is all it is?"

"Sure." She declined any extra money. With her spirits partly restored Mrs. Pakara proceeded to pack the dress almost reverently into a cardboard box which she tied with gift cord. "Now we have tea," she said.

She led the way into the room where the baby had lain. It was strangely quiet without him.

"No baby?" asked Laurel with a sense of disappointment.

Mrs. Pakara shook her head violently and knelt to the charcoal fire in the centre of the room heating the kettle. "Not want to talk about it," she said, and scuttled to the sliding cupboards to produce crockery and plates of home-made delicacies.

Laurel watched, perplexed, and worried at the little woman's obvious distress.

"I hope nothing has happened to the baby," she said.

Mrs. Pakara again shook her head as she measured tea from a canister into the teapot. "Not know."

"You mean the baby is missing?"

"No gone away."

Mrs. Pakara made the tea and passed a cup to Laurel. "You mean the baby is not coming back?"

She shook her head and passed the cakes. They munched and drank their tea in silence until Laurel had to say something, for the woebegone little face disturbed her greatly.

"Would you not like to tell me about it? Perhaps I can help."

Mrs. Pakara folded her hands meekly in her lap and stared down at the glitter of her rings. "Daughter-san very pretty, very talented. Wanted daughter-san to go to university, perhaps to America to learn more. But daughter-san headstrong. Wanted to be Geisha girl." Mrs. Pakara lifted shiny black contemptuous eyes. "Geisha girl is described as being an entertainer. We know how many geisha have become the playthings of rich men and are concubines. Tell daughter-san this, will not listen. She go for glamour." Mrs. Pakara shrugged narrow shoulders. "Daughter-san go with one rich man long time, have baby son. Rich man not know of son. But rich man's wife find out. Wants to adopt baby of husband. Daughter-san say no."

"Poor child," Laurel said sympathetically. "But your daughter cannot hide forever. She will need money. Can I help?"

Mrs. Pakara shook her head.

"Has your daughter considered how much better off her baby will be with the rich man's wife? He will be educated, and what's more important, he will have a name."

"Daughter-san never give baby away."

"Maybe my husband can help. Talk to this rich man's wife and make her understand."

"Rich man's wife not understand. Not had any babies." Terror shone in her eyes. "Not tell husband – promise!"

Laurel leaned forward and patted the quivering hand. "I promise, and don't upset yourself. Something will turn up, I'm sure."

"Turn up?"

Laurel smiled tenderly. "I mean something might happen to help your daughter."

Mrs. Pakara shook her head. "Rich people very powerful."

128

When it was time for Laurel to leave for her appointment at the hairdressers, the little dressmaker seemed brighter. She rang for a taxi and Laurel left after offering to help in any way she could. Mrs. Pakara, with tears in her eyes, thanked her.

Her small tragic face was before Laurel's eyes as the taxi racketed along. Most taxi drivers in Tokyo drove like mad, impervious to oncoming traffic. But Laurel was much too pre-occupied to notice. During the time she was in the hairdressing salon she thought about the delicious little Fusako, saw him again bowing before her, bottom in the air as his head came down to touch the floor between his chubby hands.

She hoped fervently that something would turn up for daughter-san to help her in her dilemma. Her taxi driver had promised to pick her up at the end of her appointment and she waited outside the Imperial for quite a while. When it was evident he was not coming, Laurel was thinking about stopping another when Dennis Summers drew up in his neat grey car.

"Hello," he said, all smiles. "And here was I thinking that this was my unlucky day. Hop in, I'll take you to lunch."

Laurel stood clutching the cardboard box containing her dress. "I'm sorry, Dennis, I must go home to lunch. Kirk will be expecting me."

He frowned in mock dismay. "Are you afraid of him?"

Laurel regarded his wry grimace and realized he was challenging her to go with him. Any other time perhaps she would have done. But after lunch she would have to get ready for her visit to the Palace and she wanted everything to run smoothly.

"I'm sorry, Dennis. I simply have to be back because I'm going to the Imperial Palace this afternoon."

He had opened the car door and she made no attempt to

get in. He looked gay and uncaring and she tried to remember when she had looked the same – or would ever look the same again?

Dennis leaned forward. "You look very worried. A pretty girl like you should never be worried. Besides, I owe you an apology for behaving so disgustingly at your housewarming. Surely you aren't going to deny me the pleasure of taking you out to lunch to aplogize?"

"You don't need to apologize, Dennis. You didn't do anything unmannerly."

"If you don't come with me for lunch I shall conclude that you haven't forgiven me."

"Dennis, don't be an idiot. Look, I must get a taxi."

He shrugged resignedly. "All right, you win. Hop in and I'll run you home."

Still Laurel hesitated. "If you're on your lunch hour I shall make you late unless you stay to lunch."

He reached out for the box she held and tossed it into the back seat. Laurel slipped inside and he set the car off at speed.

"It's very kind of you," she said. "I'm not exactly wild about using a taxi. They remind you too much of life insurance. I don't know what happened to mine. He did promise to pick me up at the Imperial Hotel."

He grinned at her. "Probably lost his way. I've never met one yet who knows much more than half a dozen addresses."

The next moment she was leaning forward and peering through the windscreen. "There he is, coming this way."

She waved and the taxi driver nodded as he flashed by.

Dennis said dryly, "Looks as though he picked another passenger up on the way. You can hardly blame him, since they're paid by the number of fares they pick up."

Laurel sighed. "I don't feel so bad at not waiting any longer. I paid him for the return journey."

130

It came to her with a small unpleasant lurch of her stomach that they were not going in the direction she had expected.

She laughed. "Talking about taxi drivers, are you sure this is the right way to Sakura?"

He grinned. "I'm taking you to a Swiss restaurant specializing in Swiss cuisine. You'll enjoy it and it's much quicker than taking you home. We're here now, so don't argue."

He pulled into a driveway threading among smooth lawns to brake outside a Swiss-designed eating place with the chalet verandahs filled with flowers and alpine scenes painted on the walls.

Laurel, hiding her dismay, gave in gracefully. After all, Kirk might not have gone home to lunch either, but she had to phone to tell Reko in case he was worried.

Kirk had not arrived for lunch when she phoned Reko, to say she was having lunch with a friend. The meal was one of gastronomical delight. Along with her companion's flattering remarks and open admiration it gave poor Laurel a sense of pleasure after Kirk's casual treatment. Dennis knew how to entertain a woman and bring the best out in her.

Granted he worked on blatant flattery, but it was balm to her sore heart. He might have been serious in his gratitude to her for what she did for him at the housewarming party, or he saw it as a successful line of approach as he angled to ingratiate himself into her good books.

Whatever it was, Laurel refused to dwell upon it and set out to enjoy herself. She was almost sorry when it was over and Dennis was running her home.

"We must do this again," he said rather too casually. "Anyway, I'll be seeing you at the weekend when we go to Mount Fujiyama."

They both saw the long opulent car parked on the drive of the house when Dennis turned in at the gates.

"The lord and master is home," he observed cynically. "I won't stay." He grinned down at her. "Did you know your husband is an expert at judo and karate? He holds a black belt. Farewell, fair maiden. I must dash."

He pulled up to give himself enough room to reverse and raising an arm to Laurel as she left the car, he was soon away. Laurel entered the house knowing that Kirk would not be pleased at her dining with Dennis. She grew meditative, realizing she did not exactly like Kirk dining with Nina. So it was with complete sangfroid that she entered the dining room to see Kirk still seated at the table.

The casual way in which he put down the newspaper to regard her with those keen grey eyes sent a wave of colour to her face. She was determined to treat the whole thing lightly, yet here she was, feeling caught out as regards herself.

"Did you enjoy your lunch?" he asked casually.

His eyes roved over her flushed face, the becoming hairdo and her pretty powder blue silk suit. A suspicion of a smile hovered around his lips.

"Very much," she answered lamely, taking off her gloves with her shoulder bag in place.

He leaned back in his chair stretching out his long legs and continued to gaze fixedly at her face.

"Who was the friend?"

"Dennis. Dennis Summers."

Laurel had advanced into the room to halt a few feet from the table. For some reason she felt glued to the spot. She had the feeling of a child facing an irate parent, for Kirk's eyes had narrowed to pinpoints of steel.

"You're not to dine with Dennis again alone. Is that understood?"

He continued to look into her face and something like a flash of sword play passed between them.

Laurel was momentarily staggered. "Why not?" she asked,

the gloves lying limply in her hand.

"Because I say so," with provoking calmness. "Dennis Summers is a menace no husband wants to deal with as a companion for his wife. His reputation concerning his affairs with women since he came here is not commendable. He spends most of his free time between geisha houses and the wives of English settlers here."

"Then why do you have him for a friend?"

"Because his job as manager of one of the big international banks in Tokyo gives him the privilege of moving freely in society."

Laurel bit her lip. "I see. I had a suspicion of his being that kind of man. But I can take care of myself."

Kirk raised his eyebrows slightly. "You can't mix with shady characters without some of the slime rubbing off on yourself. I want your word that you will not go out with him again nor entertain him here on his own. If Jean is with him it doesn't matter. The man may seem harmless to you, his type usually do. I assure you he is not."

Laurel fidgeted with her gloves, compressed her lips and raised her eyes. He was looking at her with an expression which stirred her pulses profoundly.

"Well?" he asked at last, his charming smile full of that winning quality which made her like putty in his hands.

Even so it could not abate the feeling she had regarding his own association with Nina. Her deep breath was a call-up for all the fighting spirit she possessed.

"What about your association with Countess Nina? You dine with her."

She was unconsciously standing rigid, meeting his eyes with the gleam of something like war passing between them. He rose to his feet and walked to the window before turning to face her.

"I thought we'd settled that when I assured you that there

133

was nothing between us." After a significant pause, he added with the slightest inflection of a taunt in his deep voice, "You're not jealous, by any chance – are you?"

Laurel dropped her eyes and bit her teeth together hard. She was jealous, terribly so. On the other hand he must never know. She could bear anything but that.

"Why don't you look at me? Are you afraid?"

Laurel took her courage in both hands and lifted her face to look him in the eyes. "No, I'm not afraid."

In that moment, like a blinding flash of light, came the realization that she had left her dress in Dennis's car. Seeing Kirk's car on the drive had driven it completely out of her mind. Her hand flew to her mouth in dismay.

"Oh, my goodness! My dress! I left it on the back seat of Dennis's car. He won't notice it."

The next moment Kirk had strode from the room. Laurel closed her eyes. The sound of his car dying away in the distance was like the tail end of a hurricane which had swept through the house leaving her limp and exhausted.

She went slowly to her room, dragging the shoulder bag down and swinging it along lethargically, too spent to care what Kirk might say to the hapless Dennis.

Laurel was ready when, at three precisely, the long black limousine with the Imperial coat of arms slid up to the front door. Kirk had successfully retrieved the dress, leaving it with Reko and going off at speed without a word to herself. To be fair, he could not be blamed for that. The errand had made him late reporting back to work and he would hate that.

She would have liked him to have seen the dress, though it was just as well he had not. He would hardly have been in the mood to give an unbiased opinion. Nevertheless, as she took a last look at herself in the dressing table mirror, Laurel saw no flaws in her appearance. The small tiara in her beautifully dressed hair was perfect above the dream of a dress, giving her the feeling of being a fairy-tale princess in full regalia.

A black-liveried driver stood impassively beside the open door of the car, closing the door behind her after she had slipped inside. The car purred along on its luxurious springs and the feeling of it all being a dream continued during the drive. White swans glided silently on the tea green waters of the moat surrounding the palace as they passed over the bridge through the Ohte gate and on to the grand entrance door.

A master of ceremonies awaited her in the entrance hall. He bowed low over her hand as she presented her card, another liveried footman came forward and she was conducted to a charming powder room. In this charming dressing room of wall-length mirrors pretty girls in fabulous kimonos fluttered around her like dainty butterflies to take her wrap.

They gazed down in open admiration at her dress and lovingly touched the smoothness of her hair for stray strands, caressing the tiara like an open flower. Laurel's smile was as warm as theirs when they bowed her out to where the master of ceremonies was waiting. Another deep bow and she was escorted along corridors of endless length, though strangely cheerful. Spaciously, lined with beautiful aromatic wood, they were enclosed with glass walls through which one could see courtyards, gardens, bamboo bridges over streams, flowering shrubs and pagodas. And there were flowers everywhere.

At last they halted outside a door and Laurel was shown into a room of fantastically muted colour. Most of it came from a bower of Western and Japanese flowers artistically arranged in the centre of the room.

Fabulous silk furnishings, gilt chairs and divans upholstered in Kyoto silk and lacquer cabinets filled with objets d'art lined

135

the walls. The light and spaciousness of the room was again enhanced by the view through the sliding glass walls opening on to the gardens. Laurel had the sensation of being in an underwater cavern of sheer shimmering beauty.

Cherry trees heavily laden with blossom were among fountains sending up jewelled sprays in the sun. The ladies of the court, assembled in the room in their beautiful kimonos, were not unlike flowers themselves. There was about a dozen in all, talking and laughing quietly as she entered.

Countess Nina detached herself from a small group and came to greet her coolly. Laurel felt she was doing what she had to because she had no choice. Laurel was introduced to countesses, ladies and others with no title. Those who could speak English did so, the others smiled intelligently and drew her warmly into their circle.

Soon they were all trooping out of the room behind a liveried servant to follow him along more corridors to a room in a picturesque courtyard. The laughter and whispering among them ceased when the servant admitted them into a room where deep red roses and white orchids made splashes of colour against crimson silk drapes and neutral walls.

Here again was a view of the grounds through the sliding glass walls. As they stood in silence waiting, the Empress, a sweet doll-like creature, entered. Everyone bowed as she walked to a beautiful sofa where she sat down. When Laurel was presented to her, her almond-shaped eyes danced as she wished her a happy marriage and many sons.

Laurel sat beside her on the sofa for tea and the Empress asked endless questions about London. She had the most enchanting laugh, the quietest of voices, and her dainty mannerisms were all the more fascinating because of her excellent English. Her kimono was white with a blue and silver obi around her small waist. Her beautifully dressed hair was crowned with a tiara of magnificent stones. Laurel was entranced.

She was still bemused by all the splendour when the tea was over and the ladies were trooping once more along the corridors to the reception hall. Suddenly her heart missed a beat. Kirk was there, tall, hatless, dark-haired and standing with an easy grace as he talked to the master of ceremonies.

His devastating charm, his sense of humour, his good looks and his congenital gift of adapting himself to anyone bound him to her in unbreakable cords. Nina greeted him first as one who had the right to.

"Kirk, how nice to see you! You have come to collect Laurel?" she murmured with a smile specially reserved for him.

A faint flush stained her cheeks as Kirk greeted the woman warmly before giving his attention to herself.

"Ready, Mrs. Graham?" he said, raising a brow as he looked her over. "You look lovely."

A few words with Nina, who had scarcely glanced in Laurel's direction after Kirk's praise, and they were off.

"How did it go?"

Kirk had cleared the palace grounds and was now driving carelessly, easily along the main road. Laurel did not answer immediately. She was remembering his gay smile at Nina and the woman's face at the sight of him. A light had been switched on behind the mask and lovely slanting eyes. Her throat worked spasmodically and her words came forth on a gigantic effort.

"I enjoyed it all immensely. The Empress is delicious and I wouldn't have missed it for worlds."

He said airily, "You'll be seeing more of the palace when the Emperor returns. However, I want you to relax most of the time for the present. The entertaining, apart from the essential engagements, can be shelved until later." He tossed her an engaging smile. "You're doing very well. Nina will be a great help to you in introducing you into the scheme of things. She's a good horsewoman and will be a companion for you when your horse arrives."

Laurel felt herself stiffen, though she kept her voice steady.

"I'm not sure whether Nina and I have that much in common."

He let a moment or two go by. Then: "Why not?"

Laurel moistened dry lips. "Some women prefer men friends, and I think Nina is one of them."

"But you hardly know the woman."

She fixed her eyes on the road ahead and compressed her soft lips.

"I'm sorry, Kirk. I have the feeling that Nina is about as eager for my company as I am for hers. Besides. . . ."

"Besides what?"

His voice was clipped with displeasure, sending a tremor through her. She clenched her hands in an effort to subdue it.

"I . . . I don't want a woman companion. A married couple should be sufficient company for each other without a third party."

"I agree." Kirk sounded like a man being reasonable against his will. "Circumstances, however, alter cases. You've left behind all your friends and acquaintances. Here you're a stranger with no real friends as yet. I'm not attempting to find you friends, I'm merely suggesting you cultivating the right kind of people. By that I mean those in my own particular sphere."

"I shan't let you down by becoming entangled with the wrong people," she said bitterly.

She felt rather than saw the tightening of his jawline. "You're being deliberately awkward. I don't know what's got into you. I don't suppose it's occurred to you that I shall be
138

away at my job all day and there'll be nights too when I have to be on duty. I don't want you to be too much on your own."

"I'm intelligent enough to fill in my time without becoming bored. There's so much to do here and to see. I can join the library and go to flower arrangement classes."

He said no more, but the shutter was down firmly between them. They were turning in at the drive when he said in an off-hand way, "I shall be busy for the next couple of days, so this will be our last evening together for a while. Shall we dine out, or are you tired?"

Kirk had drawn up at the door, shut off the engine and turned to look down at her. While he looked immensely fit and virile, to Laurel's loving eyes he also looked fatigued and much too lean. He looked as though he was under a great strain. Instantly she put it down to his seeing Nina again.

He was resenting her being where Nina ought to be, by his side. I'm a coward, she thought fleetingly. I ought to have it out with him here and now, end his torture and mine. But I can't. Not yet. I love him too much to lose him, even without his love.

"No, I'm not tired. I'd like to go out to dine if you don't mind."

Did he seem relieved? Laurel stumbled from the car. Wildly, she wanted to fling herself into his arms and beg him to stay at home. But the intimacy of an evening together would be too big a strain for them both.

"Have a good rest," he said. "It will freshen you up for the evening."

She nodded and walked blindly indoors to her room.

CHAPTER TEN

Tokyo had everything to offer in the way of excellent cafés, restaurants and eating places, often in beautiful and luxurious settings. Kirk drove out that evening to a place set in many acres of exotic gardens. Tables were set outdoors beneath gay lanterns, tinkling fountains, shallow streams stapled by bridges, pagodas and rock gardens.

After parking the car, they were conducted to a table near a picturesque pagoda by a kimonoed lady who gave them hot towels to wipe their hands and face and large white aprons to put on before they sat down. In the centre of the long table, which seated six people, a brazier was heating iron bars, which the pretty cook was brushing with oil.

The beef steaks she laid on them were done to a turn and handed around to the diners. The meal was leisurely with endless courses. After the succulent beef, there was veal, sweet corn, lotus root and so many more delectable dishes that Laurel lost count. Eating with chopsticks made dining a leisurely and more enjoyable thing, for in slowing up the process, the food was given time to digest because it was not crowded into the stomach.

Thanks to Kirk, Laurel had mastered the art of handling them with a light firmness instead of the rigid gripping which sent the food shooting off from between them at a tangent.

The table had filled as the meal had commenced and a Japanese couple sitting down next to Kirk greeted him cordially. He introduced them to Laurel as Mr. and Mrs. Matsu.

Mr. Matsu was an expert in marine biology and went around the schools giving lectures which he illustrated with lantern slides. He was an alert thirty-five or so with black sleek hair, high-cheekboned face and a cheerful grin.

His wife, petite, with a round baby face and very pretty smile, looked delicious in her kimono and always seemed on the verge of laughter. It appeared they were going on to a dance at the Imperial Hotel afterwards and they begged Laurel and Kirk to accompany them.

Laurel's cares were forgotten that evening, for the Matsus were an exhilarating couple to be with. Mrs. Matsu was delighted to dance with Kirk. He towered above her four foot ten like a giant and she giggled uncontrollably as they circled the ballroom together.

Mr. Matsu, at five feet six, was an excellent dancer and Laurel discovered he had a great sense of humour. It was quite late when Kirk gave the Matsus a lift home. Of course, they had to go in for a drink. The neat brown house was spotless and the little squeal of laughter coming from Mrs. Matsu as Kirk caught his head against the bronze overhanging lamp in the hall gave a happy note to their visit.

He had yet to bump his head again on the lamp in the lounge before lowering himself down on to the tatami mats on the floor. His deep chuckle as he ruefully rubbed his head mingled with Mrs. Matsu's. If the Matsus were entertaining in themselves their spontaneous laughter was encouraged by Kirk's easygoing charm. Wherever he went he brought an indescribably lightness of spirit, a natural charm, the hallmark of a good mixer.

Laurel found herself loving him more than ever in a kind of despairing sort of way. The Matsus obviously adored him. Mrs. Matsu brought out her best robin-egg blue china and the pick of her own delectable cooking, sugared fruits, tiny rice

141

cakes, deliciously flavoured, and chopsticks wrapped in colourful table napkins.

While Kirk and Mr. Matsu touched lightly on politics and culture, Mrs. Matsu gave verbal recipes for the delicacies at Laurel's request. Before they left Mrs. Matsu gave her a Kokeshi doll, a quaint little wooden doll wearing the national costume of Tohoku.

At last the Matsus had waved them off with a reluctant, "*Sayonara*" and Laurel took with her the picture of two little yellow faces wreathed in smiles and a little sad at parting.

Kirk glanced down at her with a slightly amused expression when they went indoors after putting the car away. A gleam of cynicism came into his eyes as he took in the small doll in her hand. Her sudden need for him made her breathless and weak. She wanted so much to tell him how much she loved him, and only the fear of being repulsed held her back. Scorn for her own weakness and lack of pride steadied her.

The next few days were empty ones for Laurel. She lunched and dined alone, sleeping next door to Kirk's silent, empty room. He rang up often to speak to her and let her know he would not be coming home. She hung about waiting for his ring, the sound of his deep voice. It usually came when, tired of waiting, she had gone out for a walk or to the lake for a swim. Reko would give her the message and she would long for the sound of the voice she had missed. Her walks gave her a sense of lightness and freedom, with her whole being absorbing the surrounding peace and harmony of the countryside. Laurel loved the mornings when she went down to the lake for an early swim.

The air was aromatic with fresh green crops, humidity rose from freshly tilled fields and hedges and colour mounted from deep within the valley where the brilliantly gay colours of *futons* and bed covers were spread out to air on roofs and balconies of little brown houses. The lake dazzled the eyes with sunbeamed sparks flying up from the flashing water.

In the mornings she awoke in her pretty bedroom feeling refreshed, tranquil and at peace. On the second morning several reporters arrived from the daily paper. Her visit to the Imperial palace had been noted. They were very polite and gracious, wanting to know her impressions of their country, whether she liked it and her views of the different way of life.

Reko made them tea and pictures were taken of Laurel in the garden. Then, after much bowing and many thanks, the men departed. She spent the afternoon walking in the little woods decorating the mountains with their carpets of bluebells, violets and anemones. She found a Shinto shrine gay with purple banners bearing the white chrysanthemums of the Emperor and breathed in deeply of the hedges of wild flowers lining the lanes.

That evening Jean rang up to ask her to tea the following day. Then Kirk rang, asking how she was but not asking if she missed him. His call was a brief one in which he told her to expect him when she saw him. He could have been using one of the office phones, hence his brief message. But it was poor consolation to Laurel's shaky heart.

Jean's house was a sprawling building set in a garden. It was tastefully furnished with good paintings on delicately tinted walls and light oriental rugs. Susan was there and the conversation was mostly about the climbing expedition to mount Fuji. Their bright company lifted Laurel's spirits, but by Friday morning she was beginning to wonder if Kirk was really being delayed in Tokyo because of his work.

The morning had begun with bright sunshine which Reko observed in a frowning scepticism.

"Sun too bright. Rain soon. Okasama not go far today."

He was clearing away the breakfast things and Laurel said

143

brightly, "I won't go farther than down to the lake!"

The sun was really hot, the sky a shimmering blue haze, and Laurel bathed for the second time that morning, lying to dry out on a towel at the lakeside. She must have fallen asleep, for a barely perceptible movement beside her awakened her with a start. The next moment a shadow moved over her noiselessly like the sun.

Laurel sat up swiftly, instantly alert to see a petite Japanese girl, chic and elegantly lovely in a blue kimono and beautiful dark hair piled high with knitting needles and ribbon threaded in it artistically. Her oval face was covered in dead white make-up which gave it the appearance of sweet serenity.

But her eyes looked tragic and haunted. The next instant she had gone, passing swiftly along the edge of the lake and round a bend out of sight. She had looked back on Laurel but once when a few feet away from her.

For her part Laurel felt she had been part of a dream which had not vanished entirely with her wakening. The sky darkened very swiftly in the next few minutes, taking on an ominous blackness, and the first drops of rain began to fall heavily as Laurel rose to her feet to gather up her things. And not a moment too soon, for the rain was coming down in earnest when she reached the house, wetting the cloud of her loosened hair cascading over her shoulders.

The house was quiet and dreamy when she went indoors wondering what Kirk was doing in that moment. Sometimes, as now, she had the feeling of him being with Nina. The thought weighed heavily in her breast as she slipped off her shoes at the back door and entered, to make her way to her room.

"Good morning," said Kirk.

Laurel's heart lurched painfully. Something like pride struggling with radiance came into her face as she tossed back her hair to look up at him. But it was in a voice cool and as soft and smooth as cream that she said,

"Good morning. So you do come home sometimes."

He had recently shaved and changed and he was lounging against the lintel of her door with an easy elegance. Apart from the tiredness of his eyes, he looked as virile and attractive as ever. Fearful of her own delight at his unexpected appearance, she scanned the dark sardonic face as if she expected it to have altered in some way.

Dimly, she was aware of his tired battered smile.

"Miss me?" he asked softly, lifting up the curtain of her hair and letting it slip through his fingers. "Your hair is like silk."

His deep voice acted like fingers plucking the strings of her heart, coaxing them into melody. It was responding madly in tune with the patter of the rain now falling in a deluge on the house. Kirk was here, it sang. Was it a trick of the morning light or did his face look thinner, more bitter?

If this was love, this hurt for him when he looked tired, the tormenting ache to see him when he was absent and the anguished longing when he was present, then she did indeed feel sorry for him too. No wonder he looked aged with longing, like herself, for something he could not have.

She said lightly, "You're here, and that's everything."

He looked down at her long slender legs beneath the towelling jacket.

"I would have come down to join you in the lake, but I had a soak in town." He grinned endearingly. "I boiled with the rest of my colleagues like a lobster in the communal baths."

"You mean the mixed bathing?"

He laughed at her scarlet face. "You must try it some time. No one takes the slightest notice of you. You just arm yourself with a bowl, soap and towel, scrub off all the dirt and jump into the cauldron of hot water." His fist made a playful feint

145

under her chin. "It's very exhilarating. Don't look so disapproving. You're in Japan, remember."

She nodded. "All the same, I think I'll swim in the lake."

"What have you been doing with your time? You're looking a lot better. Do you feel better?"

Laurel lowered her eyes from his intent look. "Yes, I'm fine. I'll go and dress for lunch."

Laurel joined him in the lounge ten minutes later. He greeted her with a charming smile, saw that she made a good lunch and having eaten his share lit a cigarette.

"No plans for today?" he asked, leaning back in his chair and blowing out a line of smoke away from the table.

"No."

"Tell me what you've been doing with your time."

She told him, and ended with tea at Jean's house. "Are we still going on the climb?"

"Yes, of course." He leaned forward to knock the ash from his cigarette. "Did you bring your riding clothes with you?"

"Yes, why?"

"Because that will be one of the items we shan't have to buy if you're already set up. We shall go three parts of the way up the mountain on horseback. It will be too tiring for you to walk up all the way."

"Can we do that?"

"Oh yes. Horses will be provided. They're big strong creatures and docile enough. Feel like shopping this afternoon? It's pouring with rain, but we shan't see much of it in the car."

"I never let the weather keep me in," Laurel said stoutly. "I've enjoyed walks in the rain, especially the summer rain. It's good for the complexion."

He took his time taking in the freshness of her skin, the clear eyes and pink lips. "It certainly did you no harm. You grow more beautiful every day."

146

A cool and deliberate compliment, agonized Laurel, like throwing scraps to a starving animal. He could not be so detached if he was in love with her.

With a flippancy brought on by despair, she said, "Since we're going shopping I should be making the compliments, not you."

She enjoyed the shopping spree. Kirk was humorously patient, rejecting anything he felt did not suit her and directing her choice to the more expensive range of clothes which, he said, were more profitable to buy in the long run. The rain pelted down all the afternoon and it was fun holding hands and dashing through the deluge to the shops.

In the course of the afternoon they strolled into a fashion house to find a show of fashions in progress. Kirk bought several of the really beautiful model dresses, suits and beach wear for Laurel.

"Wear that peacock blue thing for dinner this evening," he commanded.

It was an expensive model dress, dramatic in its simplicity and hauntingly beautiful in the soft rich colours. Her slenderness carried it off as effectively as had the pretty girl who had modelled it that afternoon.

Kirk, appearing in evening dress at her door, leaned against the lintel, eyebrows raised in approval.

"Not bad," he murmured, strolling across the room to tweak the small stand-up collar embossed in pearls. His firm fingers brushed her flushed cheek, as he looked down at her clear eyes, the soft youthful contours of her face and the delightful curve of her chin.

Laurel stiffened her knees at his touch. She thought, when he comes into the room he brings something dynamic with him ... something challenging, daring and ... and exciting. His hand had dropped to her shoulder and he bent to kiss her temple lightly on the tiny scar where the vase her mother had thrown had left its mark.

She raised her eyes to his dark face, the hand resting on her shoulder tightened and a spark ignited between them. The next moment it had gone, his hand dropped.

"We're having guests for dinner this evening. Guess who?"

His mouth quirked humorously, but his eyes, those tired grey eyes which, like now, could look almost black, did not smile.

Laurel smiled. She had to. "The Matsus?"

"Clever girl! I had no idea they were back in Tokyo. They've been to Honolulu for more marine biology. That was why you didn't see them at the wedding and the housewarming. We shall entertain them in Japanese fashion. Reko has everything laid on in the Japanese room." He dropped his hand and pushed it into his pocket. "There's something else. I found a letter from Uncle George among the correspondence in my study. He's taking a holiday soon and is thinking of looking us up."

"How nice," she said, and meant it. Doctor Machelle belonged to the saner part of her life when she was a whole unto herself and not an unwanted appendage of Kirk's. "I shall look forward to seeing him. Did he say when he would be coming?"

"Actually, he's waiting for a locum to take over his practice while he is away before he can fix a date." He strolled over to the window to present his wide shoulders in evening dress. They were square and militant as though he were bracing himself to say something he found to be difficult to put across. "He's probably coming to see how I've been treating you."

Laurel stared at the back of his well-shaped head. "Why should he do that?"

A shrug. "He's very fond of you. Did you know?"

Two little vertical lines appeared between her neat brows

148

at his tone.

"I like him too, as he likes me, as a very good friend. I wish he'd marry. He's a lonely man even though he's blessed with an efficient, attractive housekeeper." Suddenly she brightened. "You know, it's only just occurred to me. They would make an ideal couple. She's younger than him, about thirty-five."

His tone was unbearably mocking. "Touché, a marriage of convenience from you! Don't tell me you're in favour of them. I thought it was only the cynics who believed in them."

"Not only cynics," she replied with spirit. "Circumstances alter cases, and your uncle George is getting on." Dead silence. Laurel wished she could see his face, but he kept his back to her and she hastened to add, "What I mean is, he's mature and past the passionate age."

Kirk turned round slowly to face her. His lips had thinned. "Do you know how old Uncle George is?" he asked evenly. "Thirty-eight. Seven years older than I am."

Her eyes widened up at him in disbelief. She was remembering the fair hair receding from the high intelligent forehead, the almost perceptible droop of his shoulders. "I thought he was nearer fifty. Why, he's almost bald!"

"His family are all the same in the male line. He married my mother's youngest sister. She died from an embolism after an appendix operation while they were on their honeymoon."

He waited for her to digest his words, his expression enigmatic.

"How dreadful," she whispered. "Poor Uncle George! I didn't know he'd been married."

She looked beyond him through the window to the garden. The rain had stopped and the sun glittered on wet leaves carching sparks from the drops of water, dazzling the eyes. A large black-winged butterfly hovered, then settled on a wad of blossom.

"Tell me," Kirk was saying, "do you regard me as past the passionate age too? After all, I'm only seven years younger than Uncle George?"

Laurel went scarlet. "I . . . of course not," she gasped, looking anywhere now but at him.

"Thanks. I'm glad of that." A pause. "You see, you would be in for a shock if you did," he vouchsafed dryly.

Before Laurel could define what he meant Reko came to say that their guests had arrived. If she had been perturbed by Kirk's last remark, she very quickly forgot it in the gay company of the Matsus. Their small faces beamed no less brightly than Reko's, who cooked and served a superb Japanese meal. Reko, in his immaculate white jacket over dark slacks, was charged with energy. All his movements were quick and light giving the impression that he, like the Matsus, had lived for this moment.

Mr. Matsu talked animatedly to Kirk on his latest discoveries in marine biology and Mrs. Matsu chatted animatedly to Laurel about the beauty of Honolulu. When their guests took their leave, Reko stood with them to wave them off.

"A delightful couple," Laurel said, when they returned indoors.

"Made for each other," Kirk observed absently as though his mind was on something else. "I'm going to the lounge to sit down and stretch my legs after being cramped up on those tatami mats." They halted at the lounge door. "What about you, my sweet? Care to join me? It's much too damp to take a walk in the garden after all that rain."

Her heart moved queerly at the challenging gleam in his eyes. They had drunk saké with their meal and the diminutive quantities they had consumed could not have made Kirk in the least inebriated. Thank goodness he took everything in moderation. Why then the gleam?

She said hurriedly, "No, thanks. I think I'll go to bed. Do we have to be up early in the morning?"

"No earlier than usual. Reko will bring you tea at seven. So you won't join me in a nightcap?" his eyes asked meltingly.

Her heart said yes, her common sense no. She shook her head.

"I really am tired after all that shopping. Thanks for everything." She had to say something.

Kirk, with dark face inscrutable, was ice cool. He gave her a long searching look. "So be it. Sleep well."

He looked grim. "I know I was afraid of something like that. That was the reason I asked you if you'd seen the baby

CHAPTER ELEVEN

Laurel opened her eyes to a morning sun caressing her eyelids like a warm kiss. She yawned, stretched her slim arms above her head and sat up abruptly. Sleep had fled and she glanced at her watch on the bedside table, thinking she had overslept. Six-forty-five.

Time to wash and dress before Reko came with her tea. He had brushed and pressed her riding clothes, polishing her boots to the sheen of glass. They were there waiting for her, along with the thick beautifully soft knitted cream sweater to combat the chills of the mountain air.

In the bathroom after cleaning her teeth, Laurel thrust out her right arm and was delighted to see that her hand did not quiver. She could hold it perfectly still. Her nerves had improved enormously since her breakdown in health. And she felt marvellously fit, thank goodness.

Kirk was in the dining room when she entered. He too wore a cream sweater and his riding breeches revealed the long supple lines of his body, giving him an indolent grace. A fugitive thought ran through her mind that she could have got up earlier and gone swimming with him in the lake.

Most husbands in the same circumstances would have asked their wives to accompany them. Evidently Kirk had no desire for her company or he would have done. Her level brows contracted.

"Good morning, my sweet. The gods are favouring us with the weather. The dip in the lake this morning was worth getting up for," he observed mildly.

"Oh!" Laurel went scarlet. How remarkable. He might have known what she was thinking.

"Alas, you were fast asleep when I looked in," he went on placidly as though she had not spoken. "The early bird catches the worm."

There was a veiled flicker of amusement in his quiet regard as he pulled out her chair at the table.

"I'm sorry. You should have wakened me."

"And scared you half to death to find a man bending over your bed?"

He sat down in his chair opposite, the amusement quickening in his eyes. There was a kind of challenge in them – a derisive gleam of laughter rousing her to instant fury. How dared he? He had been the one to remain aloof, not her. It was his place to take the initiative as a man.

"Why should I be scared of my own husband?"

"You tell me." Those grey eyes of his brought the colour to her cheeks.

She gasped, then pulled herself together. "I could never be afraid of you, Kirk," she said quietly.

"That's something anyway."

As he spoke Reko entered, bringing the savoury odour of breakfast with the tray he carried. The delicious smell assailed her small nostrils. Laurel was all at once aware that she was hungry.

They were lingering over their last cup of coffee when Jean and Susan arrived with their husbands in a station wagon. Reko made fresh coffee and they all sat down to relax over a drink and a smoke before starting on their journey.

Kirk was checking the stuff he had put into the boot of his car and Bill, Susan's husband, was talking to him when Laurel came out of the house. She had left Jean and Susan in her room repairing their make-up.

"Hello there!"

Dennis stood blocking her way, looking gay and uncaring in his riding clothes which he was obviously getting rather fat for. He was still attractive with his peaked cap set rakishly on his fair curls, but his good looks were, in the clear morning light, obviously taking a bashing from his way of life.

Laurel smiled. "Hello, Dennis, ready for our jaunt?"

He stood very near to her and spoke in a low confidential tone.

"Sorry about your dress the other day. Kirk swooped upon me like the avenging angel – or should I say devil? I'm sure his brows were winged."

"You should take up judo and karate, Dennis. You wouldn't be so scared of him then. Besides, it's good for your figure."

"Perhaps I prefer other company."

Impudent little devils danced in his eyes. But Laurel refused to take any notice of them. She had to laugh, though, at his colossal conceit in his own charms.

"You mean you prefer to span a feminine waist rather than a masculine one."

"Yes, a size twenty-two inch, should I say?" His bold blue eyes took in her small waist emphasised by her riding breeches.

Laurel laughed again. He was so ridiculous and obviously clowning. His correct summing up of her waistline, however, was proof of his experienced eye and the way it roved over the feminine figure. She would have to tread warily to keep their friendship purely platonic.

"Thanks for the compliment. I can hear Jean and Susan coming. Shall we go?"

Before Jean and Susan emerged from the house, Dennis bent his head and whispered in an urgent undertone, "Let me know when you're in town again and we can have a meal together or go to a show."

They set off, with Kirk taking the lead. Seated beside him, Laurel eyed his dark profile, her love suddenly protective.

"Climbing, my sweet, is the most relaxing of pastimes to a lover of the great outdoors. We shall spend the night at one of the stone huts on the ascent and sleep the sleep of the just. Consequently, we shall all return feeling refreshed with all the cobwebs of a week in the city blown away."

"But you've climbed the mountain before. It won't be any novelty to you."

"So I have, but only once have I seen the wonderful panoramic views of the Japanese Alps and the Pacific from the summit. It's an unforgettable sight and one few climbers are privileged to see, since Fuji is so high above the clouds that she's only on nodding acquaintance with aircraft."

"It must be a terrific height," she said.

"Twelve thousand three hundred and ninety-seven feet, to be precise. It's a little early for climbing since the top is still covered with snow, but the weather this last fortnight has been much warmer than usual for this time of the year and parties of pilgrims have been going up this month to visit the shrine at the top."

They left Tokyo behind and with it the modern world for outside the city lay the real Japan of thatched-roofed farmhouses and peasants in conical coolie hats, swatched black leggings and split-toed canvas shoes eking a meagre living from the soil. Mount Fujiyama at close quarters was a most impressive sight, a near-perfect cone rising sheer out of the plains uncluttered and free from neighbouring peaks from base to summit.

According to Kirk the climb to the summit took between seven to nine hours on foot, the descent between two and five. But they were going most of the way on horseback. Kirk had stopped in the village of Subashiri to telephone through to Ichi-Gome, the station where the climb began, to reserve horses and a guide.

When they reached Ichi-Gome the air grew much cooler, with the scent of mountain pine. The horses were waiting for them, looking strong and well fed, and after sitting down for refreshment they prepared for the climb.

At the stores an alpenstock called a Fuji-stick was purchased for each of them. It was an octagonal white pine staff to use when they reached the steep lava paths nearer the summit. The guide was quite young, around twenty, not so tall, but as strong as an ox. He cheerfully took a lot of their kit and the rest was put on a horse.

Laurel was helped on her mount by Kirk, who rode beside her as their guide went on ahead. The trail began to steepen once they left the base, meandering through pine woods which were now filled with veils of mist frolicking through the trees. It grew more dense as they climbed and Laurel felt difficulty in breathing. Presently only the trail underfoot was visible in the thick mist.

The distance between the stations seemed endless to Laurel, but she enjoyed the stop at each for tea and refreshment. Kirk had laced the tea in the flask with whisky, and snug and warm in her woolly lined sheepskin coat, Laurel felt less of the cold.

After they left the fifth station an icy wind sprang up. The trail grew steeper into switchbacks and hairpin bends and at the sixth station the horses went back. Laurel, stiff with riding in the icy cold air, was lifted from her mount and her limbs massaged by Kirk, who rubbed a cold nose against her icy one and grinned down at her.

"Well? Want to go back with them?" he quipped.

Laurel looked around to where Jean and Susan were stamping their cold feet and swinging their arms to encourage circulation. Their husbands were busy shedding their load.

Laurel's lips were parted, her throat parched with the effort of replenishing her depleted lungs with air. All the poignancy and hopes of the day had dissolved into night, icy wind biting her cheeks, Kirk's arms around her, everything strange, hurtful but sweet.

"You think I can't take it?" she said.

"No. Giving you the choice to go on or go back."

"We'll go on." His grey eyes raked her face, his arms slackened to release her. "I am enjoying it, you know."

"That's all I wanted to know. We go on to the seventh station from here. Then we bed down there for the night."

Laurel nodded, content to be taken care of by Kirk. Taking in the sweet cold air was less painful now. Behind Kirk's dark head the vast stretch of sky had changed to a deep, darkening blue and a lone star looked very near.

A star of hope? Laurel wanted it to be. In that moment it seemed worth all the heartache to be there on top of the world with Kirk. That star would shine through the years, clear and bright with a poignant pain in its wake that would never be forgotten.

Their stay at the sixth station was a short one. The air was piercingly cold and Kirk wanted to reach the seventh station early to make sure of a place on the hut in which they were going to spend the night .. Station Seven was near enough to the summit for them to rise early and reach the top in time to see the sunrise.

It was a long low building hewn out of the mountain with a roof weighted down by rocks against the force of the winds. Anywhere would have been a haven to Laurel, who was feeling the cold in her fingers and toes. All around them was the blackness of light with the lights of villages way down below twinkling up at the stars in the gloom.

She blinked at the carbide lighting in the hut as they entered to see the usual tatami mats strewn around the well in the centre of the floor, giving out warmth. Only two people were there and they had already rolled themselves up in their *futons*, the edges of which were visible beneath the curtains partitioning several alcoves from the room.

Laurel did not remember much after that. She was too tired, and was out like a light immediately she was in her sleeping bag. Jean awakened her to the light of the carbide lamp. Laurel came back reluctantly into the life of the hut from a dreamland of warmth. Her watch said two o'clock, so it was not yet dawn, and that was what they were rising at this unearthly hour for.

The men were getting the breakfast. In the fierce carbide light, Kirk looked fresh and virile as if he had thrived on the arduous climb of the previous evening. The breakfast and hot coffee laced with rum tasted surprisingly good. Laurel wriggled her toes in her riding boots, every movement painful. Before they began the walk to the summit, Kirk knelt beside her, a slightly cynical smile around his lips.

In his hand he held sandals of woven rice straw. "Fastened on top of your boots these will give you a better grip on the lava paths and they're quite durable." He grinned up at her. "You're taking it on the chin. That's what I like to see." An eyebrow lifted as he secured the covering over her boots, his keen grey eyes speculative. "Still want to go to the top?"

She looked into his dark face. The maddening stiffness in aching limbs was forgotten. "What do you think?" she answered gallantly.

Their guide, Totaki-san, gathered up and lashed together larger pieces of their equipment and, attaching smaller ones to his belt, swung the large pack on his back.

Outside the air was sweet and pure with the stars still

winking at them from the dark sky. Below them, way down below, lights came into view weaving upwards between the volcanic ash to the tinkling of a bell. Their figures showed up a ghostly white in the gloom.

Kirk said, "A party of Fuji-san worshippers making their yearly pilgrimage to the summit. They're clad in white, hence the illusion of ghosts."

He had put an arm around Laurel's shoulders and they walked to the winding path taking them upwards. Now the way was much steeper a tortuous zigzagging climb so steep in places that wire cables had been stretched besides the path to hold on to.

Kirk lifted Laurel up the steeper stretches with no sign of exhaustion. But Dennis and Susan had difficulty in getting their breath because both were overweight. After frequent rests Station Eight was reached where they rested for another warm drink.

Said Dennis in Laurel's ear, "Fuji is a wonderful sight from afar. But one is disillusioned on climbing it."

He had sat down beside her. The pilgrims had caught them up and were sitting with them enjoying a warm drink. Kirk and Jean were talking to them and Bill was massaging Susan's legs.

The warm drink was reviving Laurel, coming in between her and the cold air which made her catch her breath like diving into Arctic water. She was fascinated, even in the harsh conditions, in the vast expanse of sky. It was not black but purple, the royal rich purple of kings, a velvet mantle as befitting what the Japanese regarded as a sacred mountain.

"I find it rather wonderful," she said soberly. "Like nothing I've ever experienced before. I feel richer because of it."

Dennis jeered, "You say that now. Wait until you have to go up the rest of the way. There's a sharp incline of about thirty-two degrees that will make you long to stop for an honourable cup of tea."

Laurel had to laugh, a delightful quiet twinkle which brought several pairs of oriental eyes appraisingly in her direction.

"I'll survive," she said.

The last lap was certainly treacherous with a steepness demanding herculean efforts from heart and lungs. The wind had dropped and Kirk had hauled her against him, pushing her upwards with a deceptively careless strength. When their path had suddenly taken a U-turn over an awe-inspiring ravine, he had swept her round it before she could see the depths.

Eventually he thrust her through the last *torii* gateway to the summit. Then he went back to help the others. Jean, Dennis and Bill had come close on their heels apparently none the worse. But Susan, cold-driven and panting, almost wept with relief to reach the top.

Kirk teased her about putting on weight and suddenly there they were on top of the world with the thick clouds between them and the earth. It was like looking down into a vast snow-drift into which one could dive.

The dead silence which followed seemed almost uncanny to Laurel, who was aware of climbers joining them in large numbers. Slowly, like a vast bubbling cauldron, the clouds began to swirl and disintegrate, the sun rose slowly in a blaze of glory, tinting the heavens in a rosy glow. And then it happened. Below them, as clear as any picture could be, lay the wide expanse of the Pacific Ocean and the glorious range of Japanese Alps, uncluttered by cloud.

Cameras clicked and to Laurel's enchanted gaze Fujiyama seemed to take a bow.

"Well? Was it worth the climb?"

Kirk's voice was near her ear, his arm around her shoulders, his warm breath in her hair.

"It's wonderful," she murmured. "The land of the Rising sun."

Laurel felt chastened as they descended after peeping into the vast crater. She had only one regret. It would have been heaven to have gone through it all with Kirk, just the two of them. But one could not have everything. Maybe another time. But Laurel knew it would not be the same.

As Kirk had intimated, Laurel's visit to the Imperial Palace sparked off a number of dinner engagements at the houses of government officials. There were the usual state functions when Laurel found herself seated by someone who could not speak English too. But there was always an interpreter close by.

She was never bored on these occasions. Her lively mind and interest was caught up by the beautiful gowns and kimonos worn by the ladies and the resplendent uniforms of the men. Sometimes she would find herself seated beside famous people and would sip her champagne while lending an eager ear to their conversation, much to the amusement of Kirk.

Countess Nina was invariably present at these functions and, one evening, they were invited to dine at her home. The house in Tokyo had a spacious garden which gave the impression of being miles out in the country. The food was Japanese and her husband, Ishi, was an urbane host.

As most of the guests were European they dined in one of the Western-style rooms, high-ceilinged with cut glass chandeliers, period furniture and Japanese objets d'art, carved jade figures, Japanese dolls and priceless vases.

Laurel, seated next to her host, was captivated by his charm. There was a certain nobility of features which added to his good looks and she could not help but be drawn by his courteous manner and his obvious admiration of herself. Even Nina, scintillating with diamonds and a really beautiful kimono

161

which must have cost the earth, did nothing to make Laurel aware of her own inhibitions.

She had none that evening, for she was wearing the dress Mrs. Pakara had made for her visit to the Imperial Palace and she knew she looked her best with the small tiara in her dark hair and Kirk's diamonds at her slender throat. The shadow flitting across her face at the sight of Kirk sitting beside the woman was fleeting as she gave her attention to her host.

Her ego had a further boost when they were driving home.

"Ishi was quite attentive to you this evening," Kirk said drily. "It's not surprising, since he has an eye for a pretty woman and you were certainly one of the prettiest there."

"Thank you, she said demurely. "Ishi is a good-looking man. I like him.

"He's not a bad sort. But like most Japanese he's fond of the ladies." Kirk dipped the headlights at an oncoming car, flicked them up again and said casually, "Haven't seen any more of Dennis, have you, since Fuji?"

The unexpected question was oddly disconcerting. Laurel felt her colour rise. "Why do you ask?"

"Because you seem to like him too. I noticed you were a little flushed when you came out of the house on the morning we left for Fuji. Later, on the mountain, he was whispering in your ear and you were laughing as if you enjoyed it."

"Dennis was fooling. He's much too transparent to be dangerous."

He gave her a swift frowning glance. "That's part of his charm – or hadn't you noticed?"

"No, I'm afraid I haven't, because he isn't that important. In any case, I don't know what this is all about."

Laurel knew a sudden surge of mutiny. How dared he censure her actions? She trembled with anger and her soft lips were pressed together as she stared fixedly through the windscreen. He sounded so ... so self-righteous, when all the time he was carrying on with Nina.

"Don't take it so seriously," he said evenly. "You're sweet and trusting and you happen to have taken Dennis's fancy. I merely wanted to make sure you weren't being taken in with him. Although Japan is fast catching up with the Western world, she's still behind in issues which are taken lightly in other parts of the world. Divorce, for instance. A divorced woman here is regarded in the light of a social outcast, even by her own family, and is unlikely to have the opportunity to marry again."

"But that's awfully unfair if she's the innocent party," Laurel protested bitterly. "What about the wealthy husbands who take geisha girls?"

"The men here go to a geisha house like an Englishman might go to his club. They see nothing wrong in having another woman because they do it openly. It's a way of life. On the other hand, it does keep the wife on her toes knowing she has competition for her husband."

Laurel looked down at her hands in her lap and thought about Mrs. Pakara's daughter, the geisha girl with the delightful little boy whom she was hiding from his father's wife.

"What happens when a geisha girl has a baby by one of the patrons? It does happen, I suppose."

He shrugged as if he found the subject distasteful. "Rarely. These girls are trained and know their jobs. I believe there are some who end up as concubines."

Laurel persisted, "If it did happen could the father claim the baby has his own? Do they adopt children if they're childless?"

He smiled down at her tolerantly. "What a serious little thing you are, feeling other people's troubles as your own. Yes, a son is very often adopted by a childless couple who want an

163

heir. Boys are thought much of in Japan. There's a boys' festival on the fifth of May. On that day hundreds of paper fishes flutter from poles all over the city. The fish represents a carp, a fish that has to fight the strong currents of the rivers to exist. It's symbolic of a boy's struggles through boyhood to manhood. The shops are filled with male dolls in uniforms, in combat and in the ancient robes of feudal lords. You'll enjoy the festival."

Shall I, she thought, or will our marriage be over by then? Putting her own troubles on one side, Laurel thought of Mrs. Pakara, the dressmaker who was so upset at daughter-san's trouble with the baby, and she longed to tell Kirk about it. But she had given her word. Besides, Kirk would probably be philosophical about it.

It rained heavily that night and for most of the following morning. Towards lunch time the clouds passed and the air was still and warm. Laurel went outside into the garden, enjoying the deep intensity of fragrance after rain. She wandered down as far as the little wicket gate opening to the path leading down to the lake, and watched the clear outline of trees overladen with rain-soaked foliage leaning over the water.

Her attention was focussed on nothing in particular. Yet she was profoundly conscious of her surroundings, the perfume of flowers, the birds twittering, the pearly light over the distant hills where pines marched along the ridges like Buddhist monks on a pilgrimage. And it was there that Kirk found her on coming home to lunch.

"Penny for them," he said teasingly in her ear, coming on her so silently that she started, curiously shaken.

There was a confused awareness within her of responding to him, an awareness of feeling everything keenly, his arm around her shoulders, the deep cadence of his voice and his kiss on her hair. It was not easy to answer him with the silly pulsation in her throat until pride eased her out of the disquieting emotional spell on to solid ground again.

"I was thinking how sweet and fresh it always is after rain, like a new-minted world and a very lovely one," she said in her clear soft voice.

The face she raised to him had the ethereal quality of a pearl, her eyes were cool.

Kirk's eyes were steady, preoccupied, and Laurel wished he would not look at her so intently.

"It's been a terrible morning, yet standing here in the freshly washed air it isn't important any more." He looked up into the strangely leaden blue sky. "I can smell thunder, though. Stay put this afternoon. Don't go out. Read a book or something."

After lunch Laurel, at a loose end, wandered into Kirk's study. Sitting down in his chair by the desk, she toyed with his pen and looked around the room at the booklined walls until her eyes rested upon the smallest of the wedding gifts from the Emperor on a shelf. Laurel, recalling the card inside the box containing the bottle of saké and tiny cups, was filled with curiosity.

Why had not Kirk wanted her to read what the Emperor had written on it?

On a sudden impulse, she rose from the chair and reached the parcel down, untied the gold cord and opened the box. The card was tucked inside between the bottle of saké and the diminutive cups. With shaking fingers, she drew it out. The Emperor had written in a good hand of English.

Dear Kirk, As I regard you as both a dear friend and brother, I send you a bottle of saké without which no Japanese wedding is complete. Please use it, for then I shall regard you as being truly married. Your dear Friend.

Her hand was shaking still more when she returned the card to the box and re-wrapped the parcel. The reason Kirk had not wanted to her to see it was clear enough. He had no wish to solemnize their wedding in the Japanese way because it was only a temporary one from which he would finally seek an annulment.

Laurel paced the room, her hands clasped together in anguish. What more proof did she need? Where was her pride to stay with such a man who did not want her but who was using her for his own ends? The four walls crowded in on her suffocatingly. She had to get out to think.

The next moment she was on her way to her room to ring for a taxi. An hour or so around the Tokyo shops would clear her brain and give her time to decide what to do. Laurel was not partial to the Tokyo taxis or their drivers. Most of them spoke little English and the streets being without numbers added to the confusion. Furthermore, the drivers seemed intent upon committing suicide by the shocking way they drove.

Her practice was to wait until the taxi was approaching the place she had in mind, then tap on the window for him to stop. She had remembered seeing a small antique shop when out with Kirk, a sorrowful kind of a ramshackle building with a more resplendent shop on either side supporting it like two rich uncles. Over the door the words, "Oriental objets d'art. Please to enter," were printed in English.

All this ran through Laurel's unhappy mind as she hastily donned a white mackintosh and matching small-brimmed hat. Thrusting her legs into high white boots, she grabbed her handbag and went through the hall to wait for the taxi, smiling at Reko's look of dismay as she went.

She reached the city still in one piece, keeping her eyes skinned for the little antique shop, which was somewhere on her right close to the Ginza. Then she saw it and tapped on the window to the driver, who pulled up with a shriek of brakes several blocks ahead. Laurel paid him and walked back to the shop.

Opening the door to the chime of bells, she steppped into an Aladdin's cave glowing richly with treasures and was greeted by a small genie looking rather like a miniature Merlin. Her black kimono was sprinkled with silver moons and stars, but she was minus a wand.

When Laurel gestured that she was only looking around, the pert little face beneath a bird's nest of black hair nodded to show two gold teeth among the white ones. Laurel forgot everything including the time as she browsed among relics of old Japan, swords, face masks, old jade pieces, antique tea-pots shaped like dragons, coffee pots, shields, bronze Buddhas and fabulous obis. It was some time before she saw the pic-tures.

They were tucked away from sight in a gloomy corner as if jealously hidden from a collector's avid gaze. There were delightful sketches on wood blocks and beautiful paintings on silk.

Laurel gazed enchanted and found herself staring at the scene from the little wicket gate in the garden of her new house looking down to the lake and over the valley. The scene was identical. There it was, beautifully and faithfully por-trayed even to the winding path down to the lake. The pearly translucent glow was there in soft candy colours and there was a boat on the lake with a couple in it that might have been her and Kirk.

The lump in her throat swelled in size as memory came rushing back. Tears pricked her eyes. What a souvenir! She would always have a bit of Kirk that would always be there when everything else had gone.

"Honourable lady like?" purred the little genie at her side.

Laurel sighed. "It's beautiful. How much, please?"

The little genie stared at her for a moment and said timidly, "Two hundred and fifty yen."

"I'll take it," Laurel said delightedly.

The little genie wrapped it up neatly and gave it to her with a bow, and the door chimes echoed Laurel's pleasure as she left the shop. After making a visit to a nearby American pharmacy for a few toilet requisites, and browsing around a bookshop where she bought several magazines, she walked to a prominent corner to hail the first taxi she saw.

It was following a big car and Laurel lifted a hand when it got to within hailing distance. The next moment her hand had dropped like a stone, for she caught the sight of the profile of the car driver travelling at speed. His eyes were fixed on the road ahead. There was no mistaking that dark saturnine profile, those steel grey eyes. Kirk, with Nina beside him looking ravishing in turquoise. No wonder he had told her to stay indoors!

Her head swam. Her blood burned rushing up into her cheeks. There was a feeling and a need for something to hold on to. When the car slid beside her to a halt, she stared at it stupidly.

"Hop in before you get drowned," Dennis said cheerfully, and Laurel suddenly realised it was raining.

She slid in beside him. "Thanks, Dennis. If you'll drop me off at the first taxi rank I shall be most grateful."

"At four o'clock in the afternoon? You couldn't be so cruel!" Dennis looked affronted. "At least, have a coffee with me."

"But have you time? I don't want to be a nuisance."

He grinned and started the car. "I've always time for a pretty woman. What about the roof gardens at the Imperial Hotel?"

"All right," she said.

Even Dennis was a friend in need at that moment, someone who would take her mind off what she had just seen. Recalling his past boldness, Laurel wondered if she was encouraging Dennis into becoming tiresome, but she risked it. She was too dreadfully unhappy to do anything else.

It was pleasant in the roof gardens. Dennis did most of the talking, referring to people seated near them of importance whom he felt she should know. Friends of Kirk too, she thought bitterly, who would note her being with Dennis. But what did she care? She wondered where Kirk was going with Nina. Her heart was numb, but her pink lips were smiling at Dennis.

She refused to allow him to run her home, but insisted upon taking a taxi. Fortunately, it was the taxi driver who had taken her to Mrs. Pakara, the little dressmaker. The amazing thing about the Japanese taxi drivers was that they never forgot a face. She was carried away to arrive home in record time. The house greeted her in silence. Evidently Kirk had not yet arrived.

She washed and changed for dinner, hating the thought of seeing Kirk again and having to put on a happy face. However she tried only one solution seemed feasible. She could pack her cases and leave, end the farce of a marriage herself without waiting for Kirk to do it.

He arrived home ten minutes before dinner. Laurel had stayed in her room until she heard his car, then she opened her door and waited for him.

"Sorry I'm late, my sweet," he said, kissing her on the tip of her nose. "I won't be two shakes." The next moment he had walked off to his room.

Laurel made her way to the lounge, ashamed of herself for allowing him to play on her emotions. The glass doors in the gaily furnished lounge were closed and she walked to look

169

through them into the garden. He was late because he had been out with Nina. Yet what could she do? Tackle him about it?

Ten minutes later, he was seating her at the dining table. When he exerted his charm she was helpless. He had a way of making her feel she was the only woman in the world and the most precious. She went through an agony of longing, seeing in his tender smile a hope that if she spoke to him this evening he would tell her the truth about himself and Nina. But his first remark dispelled the hope for good.

He did not ask how she had spent her afternoon as he usually did. Instead he waited for Reko to serve the first course of their meal, then said casually,

"You remember when you went to Mrs. Pakara the first time? You mentioned a baby? He smiled at her across the table. "You also asked me whether I liked children. I do. No marriage is complete without them."

Laurel met his look gravely. She even managed a gallant little smile.

"I'm glad." She waited for him to go on.

He did not smile now. "I want to ask you about the baby you saw at Mrs. Pakara's!"

Her heart was thumping, but she had herself well in hand. "Yes. What is it?"

He looked at her squarely. "Was the baby there on your second visit?"

She gazed at him with wide eyes. "Why do you ask?"

"Because it's important."

Laurel remembered Mrs. Pakara's agitation, her fear lest Kirk should know about daughter-san taking the baby away in hiding.

"I don't understand," she said through cold lips.

"I don't suppose you do," coolly. "Well?"

It came to her then like a blinding light. The rich man, the father of little Fusako, was Ishi. Ishi Wanaka, Nina's husband. Why had she not guessed it before? But why should Nina want the baby?

She looked straight at him. It was no time for shrinking avoidance.

"Why do you want to know?" she said.

He looked at her for a moment or two in silence and waited for Reko, who had entered, to put down the hot covered dishes. When he had gone, he said,

"There's no reason why you should be mixed up in this."

Her face quivered and was controlled swiftly. "Oh, but I am if I give you the information you ask for."

He frowned. "What exactly did Mrs. Pakara say to you? About the baby, I mean?"

Laurel suddenly felt very calm. "Nina is the woman after Fuseko, isn't she? Ishi is his father."

He sat mutely considering her. "So Mrs. Pakara told you?" he said quietly.

They had forgotten the meal and were looking at each other across the table. The silence was profound.

"Mrs. Pakara did not tell me," she said with an odd vehemence. "I'm not as naïve as you appear to think. Why ... do you look at me like that? Am I not to be told anything concerning you?"

Her voice shook. Why was Kirk looking at her with a kind ... of compassion in his eyes? He looked ... sorry for her.

He spoke slowly, aware of her sudden trembling. "I'd rather you knew nothing about it."

"It's too late for that. You asked me a question. I refuse to answer it until you tell me what it's all about."

He made a gesture of distaste with a lean brown hand. "I need hardly remind you that I speak in confidence. Nina wants to adopt the baby, give it her husband's name. There'll be a

171

fine future waiting for the boy if she can do so."

"And . . . and where do you come in?"

"Nina only came for my help when all her efforts to persuade the mother to agree to his adoption failed. She's kept up a regular flow of letters to Mrs. Pakara's daughter requesting her to agree, and now she's discovered both mother and child have gone, probably left the country."

"Why doesn't Nina give her husband a son if he needs one that badly?"

"I can't tell you that."

"No? Then I'll tell you. Ishi is as yet unaware that he has a son, so Nina is counting on his delight when he discovers it. She's hoping he'll be so glad that he'll agree to divorce her so that she can marry . . . someone else." Laurel's voice quivered. She put a hand to her throat as if she was choking. Tears blurred her eyes. "I . . . I pray with all my heart that she'll never find the baby."

Then she was running from the room.

"Laurel, come back, you little idiot!" Kirk called. But she ran on to reach her room and flung herself down on the bed in an agony of tears.

"Laurel! Now do you see why I wanted to keep it from you?" Kirk was there bending over her, turning her over into his arms as he sat sideways on the bed. He had her lying across him, his face in her neck. "I knew you would be upset over the baby. Naturally, you would want it to remain with the mother."

She tried to push him away. But he had gathered her tightly in his arms. His mouth moved slowly up her neck until he found her mouth. Gradually her sobs were stifled and she grew quiet except for the thick heavy beats of her heart. Kirk's kisses were deepening. His passion was enveloping her like a furnace and her arms reached up to clasp his neck.

He laid her back on the bed to take her lips with a roughness that was dearer to her than tenderness. Then there was an urgent tapping on the door. Kirk said something explosive, released her reluctantly and was on his feet, straightening his tie and smoothing back his hair.

"What is it?" he cried, and strode to the door.

It was Reko. Kirk closed the door behind him and she heard their voices receding. Laurel saw Kirk no more that night. He was out when Reko brought her hot milk at ten o'clock.

CHAPTER TWELVE

LAUREL'S mind was firmly made up by the time she had washed and dressed the following morning. She was going to leave Kirk. His compassion had urged him to follow her to her room in an attempt to comfort her. His lovemaking had meant nothing to him. He was sorry for her and probably a bit ashamed of using her for his own ends.

Furthermore, he had ordered Reko to doctor the milk she had taken the previous evening to give her a sound sleep. Why else should she go out like a light after she had drunk it? Consequently, she had overslept, which had its advantages since she was too late to have breakfast with Kirk.

It was half past nine when she went to the dining room, where she waived breakfast in favour of a little toast – and she had to push that down. There was the usual pile of Japanese and English morning papers on the table and she looked among them uncaringly.

Laurel could not read Japanese, but the word geisha caught her eye.

"Reko!" she called him from the kitchen, and gave him the paper folded against a column, just a brief announcement. "Please tell me what this says."

Reko read it, silently, then lifted a grave face. "Geisha girl jumps into crater of volcano with baby son." He shook his head. "Many suicides in Japan. Many young ones."

"Yes," Laurel said impatiently. "But what is the geisha's name?"

He lowered his eyes and read aloud. "Kiki Pakara, number one geisha, and Fusako-san, baby son."

Laurel closed her eyes and the tears trickled through her lashes. Reko was concerned, but she waved him away, shaking her head, and he left her alone with her grief.

So Laurel cried, for Mrs. Pakara who had lost a beloved daughter and grandson, for Kiki whose only sin was being young and headstrong, for Fusako who had bowed to her so deliciously, then toppled over with chuckling. For Kirk whom she had loved and lost.

When she was more composed, Laurel went to her room to bathe her eyes and order a taxi to take her to Mrs. Pakara to see if there was anything she could do. But the little brown house was all locked up and deserted.

Fortunately, Laurel had asked the taxi driver to wait, so she returned to the house. Passing the lounge she smelt tobacco and peeping in stared in utter surprise.

"Doctor Machelle!" she cried, going forward to greet him warmly.

Kirk's uncle George took her hands and kissed her cheek. "How are you, my dear? And how do you like being married?"

Laurel's smile did not reach her eyes and he noticed her swollen eyelids. "Has Kirk been beating you?" he asked wryly. "You've been crying, haven't you?"

She nodded. "A tragedy in the morning paper upset me. I knew the people concerned."

He nodded sympathetically. "Hard luck." Then he shook his head at her ruefully. "You take things too much to heart, my dear. I'm sure Kirk thinks so too."

Her smile was still sad. "It's the way I'm made. I'm so glad to see you, and I know Kirk will be too."

"I've called to see Kirk at his office. He'll be home as soon as he can arrange it." He looked appraisingly around the pretty

175

lounge with the charming view of the gardens through the sliding glass windows. "You have a delightful house and gardens. The Japanese have the right idea. They derive great joy from nature!"

Laurel listened, her thoughts in a whirl. The Doctor's arrival rather complicated matters, although she was glad to see him. The thought occurred then that she might even travel back with him to England.

"Would you like to see over the house?" she asked cordially.

"I would indeed. Reko has taken my cases to a guest room. I thought it charming."

Laurel slipped a hand through his arm and escorted him over the house. He was delighted with the garden and the view over the valley and the lake.

They walked down to the lake through the little wicket gate. The doctor asked permission to smoke and took out his pipe as they strolled down the slopes.

Smoking contentedly, he asked, "How have you been keeping?"

"Very well on the whole."

"Earthquakes upset you?"

"Nobody enjoys them, but I shall get used to them in time."

Laurel felt a wariness in his voice and manner and remembered that he had seen Kirk before he came to the house. She looked across the lake to the distant hills shimmering in the morning sun, their peaks softened by blue shadows against a bluer sky. How lovely it was! She had forgotten for the moment that she could soon be leaving. Her heart twisted queerly at the thought of it. Doctor Machelle was saying,

"I haven't been here since I was in my teens. I've found it changed a lot. The total disregard of the people strewing rubbish around their parks amazes me, and they've become Americanized, which is a great pity, although I never was one for sitting *à la japonaise*. It's much easier for a man who's putting on weight to use a chair. Kirk takes it all in his stride, but then he's so amazingly fit and energetic. I'm afraid I was a little hard on him when you came out here."

Laurel felt suddenly very cold. "What do you mean?"

"Shall we sit down and talk?" he said. They had reached the lakeside and he motioned to a wooden seat set among black trees splashed with persimmons. They sat down. "I told Kirk you were coming out too soon after your illness, that you needed at least a year for convalescence. I sent you out to him on condition that he went easy with you and stressed the fact that you weren't to have any children for at least a year."

Laurel took what he said in slowly, trying to stem the wild hope in her heart. Then she remembered her last conversation with Kirk and his refusal to take her into his confidence and the reason for Nina wanting to adopt the baby.

"I wonder . . ." she broke off abruptly.

"Go on. Finish what you were about to say," Doctor Machelle said urgently.

"I'd rather not," she said stubbornly, and twisted her hands in her lap.

"I think you had. This could be very important."

She composed herself. "Kirk and I have separate rooms, have done since our marriage."

"Good heavens! My dear, I'm most dreadfully sorry. You see, I'm to blame. I told Kirk about woman patients of mine who, on marrying too soon after a nervous breakdown, had conceived almost right away, with disastrous results."

"But I'm not the neurotic type. I've never been nervy. I've always been healthy. You know that." She looked at him in bewilderment.

He nodded. "I'm sorry. The frustration of being near the man you love and not belonging to him couldn't have helped

177

in your recovery. I see that now." He smote his knee with a clenched hand. "I wish I'd kept my mouth shut." He looked so abject.

Laurel generously patted his hand. "Don't distress yourself. It wouldn't have made any difference to our relationship. You see, Kirk is in love with someone else."

"He's what?" Doctor Machelle exploded. "You're joking!"

She removed her hand from his to push back her hair from her forehead wearily. "No."

"Nonsense! Why, Kirk was determined to have you – I know that. I'll have a talk with him."

Laurel shook her head violently. "Oh no. Please, Doctor Machelle. This is between Kirk and myself."

He patted her shoulder, said gently, "I'm your uncle George too, my dear. Can't you call me that?"

"Uncle George, then. Please don't interfere. Kirk must do what he feels is right for his happiness. I love him too much to see him unhappy."

"He doesn't know how lucky he is, the young scamp. I suppose you're sure about this other woman in his life?"

Laurel nodded. "Please don't ask me any more about it. I don't want to discuss it."

"Have you thought about yourself? What are you going to do?"

His arm had moved around her and Laurel stiffened. "Shall we stroll back?" she said. "It's getting on for lunch time."

He put out his pipe and returned it to his pocket as if he had lost the taste for it. "You're not angry with me for doing what I have?" he asked as they strolled back up the incline.

"Of course not. How could I be since you acted in my interests as a doctor should?"

Laurel smiled at him, but she did not take his arm as she had on the way down to the lake. A feeling she could not describe had come over her from the moment his arm had slid around her waist. Something Kirk had said returned to her, filling her with apprehension.

They had reached the little wicket gate leading into the garden when the doctor put his hand on her arm and looked down fixedly at her.

"You know, don't you?" he said quietly.

She lifted a clear gaze. "Kirk told me you were fond of me."

"Fond!" His laugh held no mirth. "I worship you. I hope you'll forgive me, knowing that."

Laurel was touched. "Oh, Uncle George, I am sorry."

She smiled at him tenderly and he turned away.

"You make me feel so ashamed. You're so sweet about it – and I deliberately tried to wreck your marriage."

She laughed lightly. "Forget it. Come on, we shall be late for lunch."

He hung back and gripped the top of the little gate. "You won't be so ready to forgive when you know the whole truth."

"But . . ." Laurel began.

He cut in sharply, gazing down at his white knuckles. "I set out to deliberately wreck your marriage. I hated Kirk's good looks, his charm and easy way of collecting all the best in life so casually. I told myself that had he not come on the scene when he did, you and I would have eventually come together."

Laurel was staring at him in wide-eyed bewilderment. "I can't believe it!"

"Why did you think I had you at my home to look after you? A doctor doesn't usually take his patients in and take full responsibility for their recovery unless there's a very good reason."

"Don't tell me any more, please."

She turned and walked to the house, leaving him to follow. At the door of the house she paused for him to come beside her.

"Kirk mustn't know a word of what you've just told me. Everything that's passed between us must be forgotten." She had a sweet dignity which emphasized her youthfulness. Her smile was wistful. "Let's forget about it. I want you to enjoy your stay here."

She almost added that she would most likely be going back with him. But she knew in the face of what he had told her that this would never be. She would travel alone.

Kirk did not come home to lunch. There was no word from him, so they dined together. It was not much of a success, Laurel tried too hard to make it so. The doctor responded as well as he could be expected to.

After lunch there was a phone call for the doctor from Kirk. When he had answered the phone, Uncle George walked into the lounge from the hall to greet Laurel, smiling broadly.

"That's a bit of luck," he said. "Kirk has got in touch with a former chief of mine who's here in Tokyo giving a series of lectures. No doubt you've heard of Paul Glennock, the famous brain surgeon? He wants me to meet him this afternoon at his club, then go along to listen to a lecture. He's sending his car for me."

Laurel was as relieved as he was. "How nice," she said. "I know you'll enjoy it."

When Uncle George had gone the house seemed silent and empty. Laurel dressed for dinner that evening thinking ruefully that even his company was preferable to none. Kirk had not rung up or put in an appearance and she went into the lounge half an hour before dinner to leaf through a magazine.

She had been in the lounge ten minutes when the slam of the car door heralded his arrival. Her heart began to beat in thick heavy strokes as she heard his deep voice mingling with Reko's lighter tones.

The next twenty minutes were the longest she had ever lived through. She sat facing the garden trying to pluck up enough courage to face the final scene which would decide everything. Laurel knew with a sinking heart that Kirk had probably got Uncle George out of the way to that he could talk over their future.

Outside in the perfection of a summer evening, the little birds were singing lustily and the large-winged butterflies fluttered among the flowers, as her heart fluttered when Kirk came striding in the room. He strode in with an easy grace and a gleam in his eyes which made her heart turn over.

Poor Laurel had never seen him so happy ... so virile and so utterly handsome in his evening dress. He laughed down at her, told her he was hungry having missed lunch, and teased Reko who struggled with the bottle of champagne which refused to open until Kirk took it in his strong brown fingers.

Laurel stared at the champagne, tried to laugh lightly back and avoided his eyes. His exuberance unnerved her as he filled first her glass and then his own. There was something lurking behind the gleam in his eyes which she was unable to define ... something that tingled and sparkled like the champagne.

She had never made him so happy. Lucky, lucky Nina! Then he was looking at her teasingly, saying with a humorous tender laugh, "Come on, eat up. You can do better than that!"

When he rushed her to the lounge after dinner, Laurel was aware of an approaching climax. Then Reko followed them in with the Emperor's wedding gift in his hand. Kirk thanked him and he withdrew.

Laurel was sitting on the settee as though hypnotised as Kirk unwrapped the gift and brought forth the bottle of saké and tiny cups. Solemnly, he filled the first of the three tiny cups with three distinct pours. Then he raised it to his lips

181

and took it down in three sips. He refilled the cup in like manner again for Laurel and, as he passed it to her, he looked deeply into her eyes and she understood. She drank it in three sips as he had done.

The second cup was now filled, Laurel having it first before he had his. The third cup he took first and she took the second. By this time her face was sweetly flushed, her eyes were like stars ... and Kirk was looking at her as if he was having difficulty with his breathing too.

All his actions had been deliberate, and the last in which he inexorably drew her up into his arms was the most deliberate of all.

With his lips a paper's width from hers he murmured, "Now try to get out of that one, Mrs. Kirk Graham. Our marriage has just been solemnized in the Japanese way. So you're well and truly hooked."

Up to now, Laurel had been convinced that she was dreaming. But Kirk's mouth closing possessively on her own and kissing her with all his passion unleashed was no dream. She hung on before the tempest of his kisses, loving his hard leanness against her. A long time passed before he lifted his head to look down into her eyes in the way she had longed for, as though his need of her was as great as her need of him.

"Oh, Kirk!" she said, and put her head against his chest. He felt the fragrance of her hair, the tears against his shirt front, her slim suppleness pressed against him. And he lifted her face. His lips found hers again and it was like the consummation of their marriage as they clung together, close, fiercely loving.

When sanity returned, Laurel said, "I thought you loved Nina."

"Nina?" He looked startled. "But I told you she was nothing to me."

"I was sure she was, especially when you ... you left me alone at night."

He said with disgust, "That ass Uncle George was responsible for that. He said if I had any love for you at all I would give you time to recuperate. I knew you weren't fully recovered when I sent for you. But I knew if I didn't work fast he would get you. I realize now what a fool I was to take any notice of him. I had to marry you quickly to make sure of you."

"There was never anyone else but you," she said.

He spoke forcibly, his grey eyes dark with remembered pain. "I've been through purgatory wanting you, and I was puzzled by your attitude. You were so withdrawn, so remote and trembling each time I touched you."

Her eyes refused to leave his. "Why didn't you explain about our having separate rooms?"

"Uncle George told me that he would explain to you as your doctor that it was essential for us to wait awhile before starting our married life in earnest." His smile made him so boyishly endearing, her heart reached out to him. "I'm afraid, loving you as I do, I couldn't last out. That was why I spent those nights away from you in town when I felt I was cracking under the strain. Thank heaven we're married!"

Laurel's face went rosy red. "Please tell me about Nina," she begged.

"Nina wasn't the reason I didn't come home to lunch. I was settling my affairs at the office in order to take a month's delayed honeymoon. We only had a week before because I knew I couldn't hold out much longer than that. I was giving you a month to get used to me again. But things have happened. Our married life begins as from now."

Memory stabbed like knives. Her lips trembled and there were tears on her lashes. "Poor Kiki and little Fusako. It was in the morning papers."

183

He looked grim. "I know. I was afraid of something like that. That was the reason I asked you if you'd seen the baby on your last visit to Mrs. Pakara. I knew something like that would happen if Nina persisted in her insistence on having the baby. I've been the go-between, holding Nina off and handling it with kid gloves."

Laurel thought of his telephone call that day in his study. It all added up and made sense. Kirk hugged her.

"Come and sit down," he said. He led her to the chair she had sat in earlier facing the window, sat down and drew her upon his knee. "I think I feel more sorry for Ishi, Nina's husband, than anyone else. He was terribly cut up when he heard about Kiki and the son he never knew about. He deserves someone better than Nina. Although she came from a wealthy Japanese family, she preferred the Western way of life. Her family sent her to America when she was eighteen to study at the university. Ishi was there working at the Japanese Embassy when she met him and they were married on her nineteenth birthday."

"Did she have children?"

"No, Nina didn't want children. When they came back to Japan, she was restless. Then she met a man she'd known in America, a millionaire industrialist who came over to Japan on business. They met secretly. But she was afraid to ask Ishi for a divorce. Then she discovered he had a child, a son, by Kiki. Knowing his longing for a son, she decided to get Fusako and present him to his father in the hope that he would be so delighted that he would consent to giving her a divorce."

"And she asked your help?"

"Yes. Thank heaven she's gone for good. She left Ishi and went to America yesterday to the man she professes to love." He stared out into the garden. "I'm afraid the only one Nina is capable of loving is herself. Pity, she was a charming, well-

184

bred woman and quite likeable."

"Which only goes to show that you're like the rest of the men, easily enamoured by a pretty face."

Laurel dimpled up at him and he gave a sardonic grin that consigned Nina to the depths. A sudden gleam came in his eyes as they caressed her face, a face glowing from his kisses.

"You're so right," he whispered. "I was hooked the moment I saw yours for all eternity."

His mouth was on hers, stifling anything she might have said. Passion flowed over them like an electrical storm. "I love your hair when it's in a cloudy halo around your face. I want to sleep with you and wake up in the morning to bury my face in its fragrance. I love your gentleness, your quiet laughter and your deep capacity for loving. You do love me, don't you?" he whispered urgently.

He looked down into her large eloquent eyes and found there a love and need equal to his own. His mouth tilted and she touched the corners of it with gentle fingers.

Laurel's smile was wistful. "I can't believe even yet that this isn't some fantastic crazy dream. But I know my love for you is real enough. I do love you Kirk, so much."

"And there's to be no more separate rooms?"

She shook her head.

He whispered, "Nervous?" his eyes holding hers with a mastery adding to the terrifying delight of the question.

She shook her head again, her mouth curving deliciously into a smile.

"A little," she said.

He laughed and with little devils dancing in his eyes proceeded to take down her hair.

They were late getting up the next morning with the admirable Reko bringing them tea in bed. They were having breakfast when Reko said, "I will take your cases to the car, Grahamsan. I cleaned it ready."

"The devil you did! How did you know...?" Kirk broke off, made a good-humoured gesture with a lean brown hand and winked at Laurel. "Yes, Reko, do that, and thanks."

Laurel, with stars still in her eyes, said, startled, "You're not going away again?"

He grinned across the table at her, vital and loving. "We both are, my darling. When breakfast is over, I'm going to help you pack and we're off on our honeymoon to Honolulu. I made all the arrangements yesterday."

"But ... but what about Uncle George? We can't leave a guest like that."

"It's all fixed, my sweet. Uncle George will only be too delighted to spend his holiday with Paul Glennock, listening to his lectures and going around his old haunts. He's staying at Glennock's club in Tokyo. He's coming to fetch his luggage later. I think Uncle George has delayed our honeymoon long enough!"

Laurel agreed, although she felt sorry for the man because he had loved her. Then she forgot all about him, for Kirk was looking at her and his gaze was like a kiss, promising an increasing joy forever from the endless store of their love.

THE OMNIBUS
Has Arrived!

A GREAT NEW IDEA
From HARLEQUIN

OMNIBUS — The **3** in **1** HARLEQUIN
only $1.75 per volume

Here is a great new exciting idea from Harlequin.
THREE GREAT ROMANCES — complete and
unabridged — BY THE SAME AUTHOR — in one
deluxe paperback volume — for the unbelievably
low price of only $1.75 per volume.

We have chosen some of the finest works of four
world-famous authors . . .

SUSAN BARRIE

VIOLET WINSPEAR

ISOBEL CHACE

JOYCE DINGWELL

. . . and reprinted them in the 3 in 1 Omnibus.
Almost 600 pages of pure entertainment for just
$1.75 each. A TRULY "JUMBO" READ!

These four Harlequin Omnibus volumes are now
available. The following pages list the exciting
novels by each author.

Climb aboard the Harlequin Omnibus now! The
coupon below is provided for your convenience in
ordering.

Susan Barrie

Omnibus

The charming, unmistakable works of SUSAN BARRIE, one of the top romance authors, have won her a reward of endless readers who take the greatest of pleasure from her inspiring stories, always told with the most enchanting locations.

. . . . CONTAINING

MARRY A STRANGER . . . Doctor Martin Guelder sought only a housekeeper and hostess for his home, Fountains Court, in the village of Herfordshire in the beautiful English countryside. Young Stacey Brent accepts his proposal, but soon finds herself falling deeply in love with him — and she cannot let him know . . . (#1043).

THE MARRIAGE WHEEL . . . at Farthing Hall, a delightful old home nestled in the quiet countryside of Gloucestershire, we meet Frederica Wells, chauffeur to Lady Allerdale. In need of more financial security, Frederica takes a second post, to work for Mr. Humphrey Lestrode, an exacting and shrewd businessman. Almost immediately — she regrets it . . . (#1311).

ROSE IN THE BUD . . . Venice, city of romantic palaces, glimmering lanterns and a thousand waterways. In the midst of all this beauty, Catherine Brown is in search of the truth about the mysterious disappearance of her step-sister. Her only clue is a portrait of the girl, which she finds in the studio of the irresistably attractive Edouard Moroc — could it be that he knows of her whereabouts? . . . (#1168).

$1.75 per volume

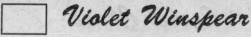

Violet Winspear
Omnibus

"To be able to reproduce the warmly exciting world of romance . . . a colourful means of escape", this was the ambition of the young VIOLET WINSPEAR, now a world famous author. Here, we offer three moving stories in which she has well and truly achieved this.

. . . . CONTAINING

PALACE OF THE PEACOCKS . . . where we join young Temple Lane, in the ridiculous predicament of masquerading as a youth on an old tub of a steamer, somewhere in the Java Seas. She had saved for five years to join her fiancee in this exotic world of blue skies and peacock waters — and now . . . she must escape him . . . (#1318).

BELOVED TYRANT . . . takes us to Monterey, where high mountainous country is alive with scents and bird-song above the dark blue surge of the Pacific Ocean. Here, we meet Lyn Gilmore, Governess at the Hacienda Rosa, where she falls victim to the tyrany of the ruthless, savagely handsome, Rick Corderas . . . (#1032).

COURT OF THE VEILS . . . is set in a lush plantation on the edge of the Sahara Desert, where Roslyn Brant faces great emotional conflict, for not only has she lost all recollection of her fiancee and her past, but the ruthless Duane Hunter refuses to believe that she ever was engaged to marry his handsome cousin . . . (#1267).

$1.75 per volume

Isobel Chace
Omnibus

A writer of romance is a weaver of dreams. This is true of ISOBEL CHACE, and her many thousands of ardent readers can attest to this. All of her eagerly anticipated works are so carefully spun, blending the mystery and the beauty of love.

. . . . CONTAINING

A HANDFUL OF SILVER . . . set in the exciting city of Rio de Janeiro, with its endless beaches and tall skyscraper hotels, and where a battle of wits is being waged between Madeleine Delahaye, Pilar Fernandez the lovely but jealous fiancee of her childhood friend, and her handsome, treacherous cousin — the strange Luis da Maestro . . . (#1306).

THE SAFFRON SKY . . . takes us to a tiny village skirting the exotic Bangkok, Siam, bathed constantly in glorious sunshine, where at night the sky changes to an enchanting saffron colour. The small nervous Myfanwy Jones realizes her most cherished dream, adventure and romance in a far off land. In Siam, two handsome men are determined to marry her — but, they both have the same mysterious reason . . . (#1250).

THE DAMASK ROSE . . . in Damascus, the original Garden of Eden, we are drenched in the heady atmosphere of exotic perfumes, when Vickie Tremaine flies from London to work for Perfumes of Damascus and meets Adam Templeton, fiancee of the young rebellious Miriam, and alas as the weeks pass, Vickie only becomes more attracted to this your Englishman with the steel-like personality . . . (#1334).

$1.75 per volume

Joyce Dingwell
Omnibus

JOYCE DINGWELL'S lighthearted style of writing and her delightful characters are well loved by a great many readers all over the world. An author with the unusual combination of compassion and vitality which she generously shares with the reader, in all of her books.

. . . . CONTAINING

THE FEEL OF SILK . . . Faith Blake, a young Australian nurse becomes stranded in the Orient and is very kindly offered the position of nursing the young niece of the Marques Jacinto de Velira. But, as Faith and a young doctor become closer together, the Marques begins to take an unusual interest in Faith's private life . . . (#1342).

A TASTE FOR LOVE . . . here we join Gina Lake, at Bancroft Bequest, a remote children's home at Orange Hills, Australia, just as she is nearing the end of what has been a very long "engagement" to Tony Mallory, who seems in no hurry to marry. The new superintendent, Miles Fairland however, feels quite differently as Gina is about to discover . . . (#1229).

WILL YOU SURRENDER . . . at Galdang Academy for boys, "The College By The Sea", perched on the cliff edge of an Australian headland, young Gerry Prosset faces grave disappointment when her father is passed over and young Damien Manning becomes the new Headmaster. Here we learn of her bitter resentment toward this young man — and moreso, the woman who comes to visit him . . . (#1179).

$1.75 per volume